Chris Trotter was born in 1981 and was brought up in Edinburgh, where he now works as a tour guide. He studied acting and tourism and is a keen photographer. Writing has been a hobby of his since he was a child, and *The Storyteller* is his first published book.

For Mum and Dad

7

Chris Trotter

THE STORYTELLER

To Joanne!

Best wishes!

Chris Trotter xxx

AUSTIN MACAULEY
PUBLISHERS LTD.

A CIP catalogue record for this title is available from the British Library.

ISBN 9781786125781 (Paperback)
ISBN 9781786125798 (Hardback)
ISBN 9781786125804 (eBook)

www.austinmacauley.com

First Published (2016)
Austin Macauley Publishers Ltd.
25 Canada Square
Canary Wharf
London
E14 5LQ

Acknowledgement needs to go to the American author, Robert Schwartz, whose books on the subject of pre-birth planning, *Your Soul's Plan* and *Your Soul's Gift*, have helped me to write this book. Thank you Robert, your books have been an inspiration to me!

Chapter One

Family Secrets

The big blue Volvo car pulled into Forest Brae campsite at exactly 2pm on a hot Friday afternoon in mid-summer.

There were four passengers: Bob, a forty-year-old car manufacturer, whose heavy bulk barely fitted into his own driver's seat; his wife Elaine, thin as a stick, with her face covered in too much make-up and sporting a series of cheap fake nails; and their two teenage children in the back; Lauren, sixteen, addicted to her iPhone, and Jamie, 13, who was…well, a 'twat' according to his sister and a 'pain in the arse' according to his father. His mother couldn't really care. All *she* was interested in was making sure she looked good. She didn't and she never would. It was too late for that; the years of alcohol abuse had taken their toll and no amount of make-up and fake nails were going to disguise that fact.

Bob was embarrassed by her. Not that he looked much better himself. He was of a large, shapeless build with an enormous beer belly, and had a chubby, but somewhat elongated face and thinning hair on top. The last time he had been to his doctor, he was told he had high blood pressure and a cholesterol level of epic proportions.

The caravan they were towing was an expensive model, but Bob had got it cheap, because he worked for the company who made it.

Bob knew everything about caravans, from the inside, underside and outside. He was obsessed with camping and campsites. Forest Brae seemed to be his favourite; after all, it was the only one they ever went to. This was their annual holiday destination, a thrilling trip to Scotland from their council house in Manchester. Jamie could hardly keep still from excitement.

The entire journey up the motorway had been interspersed with Bob going on about what he was going to do once he arrived, which they'd all been forced to listen to, as the CD player wasn't working. Lauren had her music on her iPhone, but she was damned if she was going to lend it to her brother.

At one point, Elaine had suggested 'I Spy', but Bob had scoffed at that.

"We're a little past that Elaine, don't you think?"

Elaine had gone silent again after that. She had been quiet like that for a few days now, as if something important was on her mind. She stared out the window most of the time or played with her ridiculous nails.

Jamie watched her from the back seat. He was quiet too. But then Jamie usually was. He'd learned to be; any time he opened his mouth to say anything he was either ridiculed by his sister or told to shut-up by his father. He kept his thoughts and his feelings to himself.

His thoughts at the moment were about his mother. 'What was wrong? Had she and Dad had an argument recently? Was there a problem at work? Was she as bored of Forest Brae as he was? Or was there something else?'

He looked over at his sister. Lauren was texting a friend. It always amazed Jamie that she could text anywhere, even in a moving car. Her eyes were fixated, her thumb twitching neurotically, while she chewed ferociously on a piece of bubble gum. Music leaked out through her headphones. She now blew out a huge bubble, which eventually burst with an irritatingly loud pop.

"Stop doing that!" said Jamie.

"What d'you say?" asked Lauren.

"I said, stop doing that!"

"Doing what?"

"Blowing bubbles!"

She immediately blew another one just to annoy him.

Lauren finished the text and sent it. Then she navigated back to her music list and chose a different song. She was desperately trying to distract herself from the present situation. Like her brother, she had noticed how subdued her mother had been these past few days. And that was making her anxious. She chose her favourite song, 'Common People' by Pulp.

They were common people, in a common house, living on a common street in one of the largest cities in England. She had an alcoholic mother and an irritating younger brother. She had recently split up from her boyfriend because he was a jerk and a foul-mouth, especially when he got drunk. Life, as far as she was concerned, could not be any worse.

Her father was the only person she seemed to get on with in her family. She was very much a daddy's girl; in his eyes she could do no wrong and vice versa. She didn't care that he was rude, that he loved Manchester City and that he deliberately belched loudly every time an opposing team scored a goal against them, or that he was nothing more than a builder of caravans and that his favourite food combination was chips in curry sauce. She also didn't care that he smoked like a chimney and consequently stank like one too. He was her father, and she loved him. He had brought her up on his own for several months, while her mother was in rehab, which she had one single memory of, and that was going to pick her up in the car two days before her third birthday. Elaine had been in rehab for seven months, during which time her father had survived on benefits.

Survived physically at any rate; whether his mental state had ever recovered, she didn't know. She remembered the arguments; the screaming matches between the pair of them, the sound of cutlery smashing; of doors slamming. And all this she heard while hiding under her bed with a My Little Pony clutched to her chest. She secretly resented her mother for causing her father pain. He could have chosen better.

The caravan in front suddenly pulled off down one of the lanes without indicating.

Bob thumped the horn so hard that the gobble under his chin quivered. "That has got to be one of the *worst* pieces of flaming driving I've ever seen!" he shouted.

This was rather hypocritical of Bob, as he had just pulled into the campsite without indicating himself, and along the motorway had, several times, performed some rather dangerous overtaking manoeuvres. Bob was not what you would call a patient driver and only had three points left on his licence; not that he cared.

"What did he do?" asked Elaine.

"Didn't indicate! I could have gone right into the back of him!"

"You're only going ten miles an hour!"

"That's not the point! If he can't drive properly, he shouldn't be on the road!"

"Says you who's only three points away from being disqualified!"

"Shut-up, Elaine!" was his only response.

"She's right!" said Jamie.

"I wasn't bloody asking you, was I!" snapped Bob.

When they arrived at their designated spot, Bob seemed to have forgotten about his outburst. He pulled the car to a stop excitedly.

"Here we are, kids!"

Jamie glanced out the window at the familiar view. They had been in this same spot two years ago.

Bob opened the car door and got out. The first thing he did was have a big long stretch. Then he farted loudly.

"Oh, sorry about that!"

"Dad, that's disgusting!" said Lauren, opening the boot.

Bob merely grinned. Then he clapped his hands together and said, "Right, let's get this baby set up then!"

Jamie hadn't moved. He sat quietly in the car not wanting to get out.

"What's wrong with you?" asked his mother from the front seat.

"Nothing." Then he said, "Why did we have to come back here? We always come here. Why can't we go somewhere else?"

"Because your father likes it here. And also because it's cheap; company employees get reductions here. In case you hadn't noticed we're not very well-off, Jamie."

Jamie was silent for a moment, before sheepishly asking, "Is that why you're upset?"

"What do you mean?" said Elaine.

"You've been very quiet recently."

"So?"

Jamie shrugged.

"I just thought something was wrong, that's all."

"There's nothing wrong," she said, defensively.

"I heard you arguing with Dad in the kitchen last week. You want him to stop smoking don't you?"

"You little eavesdropper; I hope your ears fall off!"

"Mum, where's the juice?" Lauren called.

"It should be in the cool bag!"

"Well it's not!"

"I don't know then, ask your dad!" Elaine came back to the conversation at hand. "I'm not upset, Jamie and certainly not because we're poor or because your father smokes, okay?"

Jamie nodded.

"Right, well don't ever bloody eavesdrop again!"

Jamie got out. Bob was busy disconnecting the caravan from the car tow, but Lauren was still looking for the juice.

"Lauren, you're a little bit in the way here!"

"I'm dying of thirst!"

"Well go and die somewhere else then."

"Lauren, sweetie, I'm going to the shop. I'll get you a Coke."

"I'll come with you."

"No, you two help your dad unpack, please. I can manage on my own."

Elaine set off for the little supermarket. When she walked in she picked up a basket and headed for the first aisle.

Shopping was the one thing in life she hated doing. It was so mundane, and it reminded her of the insignificance of her existence, of her situation.

She'd always hated mundane things and that's why she'd decided to be a stripper, if only to punctuate the dreariness, to pretend her life was exotic and exciting; to pretend that *she* was exotic and exciting. The fact was that she soon realised that she was nothing of the kind as she tried to ignore the clients' glazed stares.

But it was there she had met Bob who was a regular, and she saw him every Friday night without fail, sitting at the same table, sipping on the same drink. Bob was different though. He didn't have that glazed stare like the rest of them. Instead he would look straight in her eyes, as if wanting to say something to her, as if seeing *her* and not the stripper.

The first time she had spoken to him, he had simply asked her name. Then he had asked her if he could buy her a drink. After that she was snared; caught in his trap of charm. He was not the most handsome man she'd ever seen, but that fact didn't seem to matter.

They were married four months later in a small registry office in Manchester. The reception had been held at a dingy little two-star hotel, where they had provided a live band, probably the worst one either of them had ever heard. There were not many of Elaine's family in attendance. None of her work colleagues had turned up, and most of Bob's family and friends had ended up getting pissed halfway through the night. But none of that had really mattered.

Now, she wondered what the hell she'd done. It wasn't Bob, he had done his best. It was the drink. She was twenty-five when she married Bob. Since the age of thirteen, she had been drinking alcohol by going out to the park with her mates and huddling round a bottle of cheap cider. That was how it had started. She had grown up on an estate on the outskirts of Manchester, and everybody around her struggled with either broken homes, violence or some other kind of abuse.

She knew she was an alcoholic when she had asked an older friend to buy her a bottle of spirits when she was aged fifteen; which the girl had duly done.

She had managed to keep it a secret from Bob for the first five years of their marriage.

And then one night she had collapsed on her way back from the bathroom. Bob had called an ambulance and she had been rushed to hospital.

And there it had all come out. Her liver had just about packed in, and the doctors told her in no uncertain terms, that if she had another drink she would die.

Elaine picked up a pack of iceberg lettuce and dropped it into the basket. They were going to have a barbecue this evening, at least that's what Bob had decided he wanted.

She would buy the usual: burgers, sausages, sesame buns and ketchup. He hated relish! The lettuce was for a salad for her and Lauren since Bob didn't eat green things. She would also have to buy beer for him and soft drinks for the rest of them.

Jamie had been right; she was not herself. She was fed up with being herself. After rehab she had been fine for a few years. But the stress of it all had taken its toll on her marriage and eventually the urge to drink had become too strong again. But again, she'd got over that. However, that urge was once more raising its ugly head, and this time she was adamant it was going to be the last.

When the unpacking had been done and the tent extension had been set up, Jamie wandered off on his own.

The campsite was surrounded by forest, mostly pine trees. The landscaping was beautifully done; little trees and bushes dotted around between plots; neat signposts telling you where to go; perfectly kept grass and smooth tarmacked roads that absorbed the sun's heat.

But Jamie had seen it all before, and it bored him stupid. The first time they had come it had been a great adventure. It was all so new and exciting; the play park, the swimming pool, the gaming arcade. Now he was too old for the play park, the swimming pool wasn't as cool anymore and he'd played every game in the arcade to death. What else was there?

He watched a family outside their caravan. They had a barbecue going and the children were playing with a bat and a ball. He wished he could join them. Jamie and his sister had never played with a bat and a ball. There *was* a ball, but he had to play with it on his own. Bob had never offered to play football with him, although he was a great fan of it; and indeed it was his mother who had bought him the football for his birthday, not Bob.

Jamie really felt sometimes that he'd been born into the wrong family. Apart from football, he had nothing in common with his father. His sister was rarely civil to him and his mother…well, he really didn't know his mother at all.

The parents were watching their children happily playing, while they themselves sat on deck chairs and toasted this pleasant occasion with glasses of white wine. He knew their own barbecue tonight would be nothing like that. It would consist of his father drinking lots of beer and getting irritated with the cooking process; Lauren would sit with her headphones in and say not a word, and his mother would sit eating her salad and the occasional sausage. There would certainly be no ball games.

He reached the shower and laundry block, and was about to turn down towards the supermarket, when he saw Lauren going in with a towel under her arm.

"What's wrong with the shower in the caravan?" he asked.

"The lock on the door is broken!" she said, irritably.

"I thought Dad was going to fix that?"

"Well he hasn't, has he?!"

He followed her in.

"Lauren?"

"What now?" she said.

"After you have your shower, can you play football with me?"

Lauren stared at him.

"No!" she said, simply.

Then she turned and pushed open the door to the female showers. Jamie left the building and headed for the supermarket.

When he walked in, he went looking for his mother. He wandered along the aisles, occasionally glancing at some item that took his fancy.

Elaine unloaded the basket, one item at a time. Her stomach churned; her hands shook. It was so close. She tried stalling methods, like taking ages to find her card in her wallet and slowly packing items into the bags. Eventually though, time ran out. She took her shopping, not towards the front door, but to the counter where the cigarettes and booze were sold. She bought forty of Bob's favourite cigarettes. And then she let her eyes stray to the pocket-sized bottle of whisky just behind the assistant's head. Her heart was pounding so hard, and she was afraid someone would hear it. She tried to smile, tried to keep her voice level as she said, "And a little bottle of Famous Grouse, please!"

She watched as the assistant reached behind him and then put it through the scanner. As if in a daze she handed over the money, took that bottle and slipped it into her handbag. She had done it!

Jamie stood rooted to the spot. He had just come out of one of the aisles. He had seen!

And inside he now silently screamed. He left the store as quickly as he could. He walked back along the road as fast as possible, without breaking into a trot. He tried to ignore the tell-tale signs of panic that were rising in his gut. Signs that he so often felt.

He glanced back over his shoulder. There she was, emerging from the shop, the handbag slung casually over her shoulder. She saw him suddenly and waved. He slowed up. She smiled as she reached into one of the shopping bags and removed a can of Coke.

"There you go, darling!" she said.

Darling? She rarely called him darling. He took it from her.

"Thanks," he said.

As they walked, he swigged his Coke and pretended nothing was wrong.

But all the time, his mind was racing. That bottle of whisky could potentially kill her.

Was that what she wanted? One last taste of joy before she passed from this world into the next, if there was a next?

When they arrived back at the caravan, Elaine went straight inside and started unloading the shopping bags. Bob followed; not because he wanted to be helpful, but because he wanted to see what she'd bought.

Jamie sat down on a deckchair. Bob came back out and started pulling bits of the barbecue out of the boot and then grumbling about something. Jamie took another drink from his can. His hand shook as he raised it to his lips.

His mother wanted to be in another world than this, and now, not for the first time, so did he. He could feel his breath getting faster. He closed his eyes. What had the psychologist told him? He tried to remember now. Relax.

Take deep breaths. Steady breaths. And then he realised he was having difficulty breathing in the first place. His inhaler was inside the caravan. He went to get it. His mother was still unpacking. He sat down on the side of his bed, in the claustrophobic room and sucked in a puff of gas. He closed his eyes and held his breath for ten seconds.

Visiting the psychologist had been a sudden desperate decision. He had, of his own volition, gone to the school psychologist one afternoon during a lunchtime break, and burst into tears in front of her, saying that his dad didn't love him, his mother didn't want him and his sister teased him. The psychologist, instantly realising that the boy genuinely needed help, took him under her wing and told him to come to her whenever he needed. She had given him methods of coping with the panic attacks she realised he was having.

Jamie took another puff on his inhaler.

One of the methods she had taught him was to visualize himself in a comfortable place. Somewhere quiet, away from people.

His place was in a wood; it was dark. He was then supposed to hear something, perhaps nice music or a soothing voice. Jamie wanted simply to hear an owl hoot.

He heard it now, standing in his wood, a slight breeze rustling the trees around him. It was a barn owl. He loved barn owls. Since he was little he always had this attraction to them, ever since somebody had come to their school to talk about protecting them. He never heard them where he lived, but he once bought a CD of bird sounds and would listen to the owl section as he was going to sleep at night.

Jamie's breathing started to come back to normal. He lay down on the bed. His body still trembled.

The wood lay serene and calm around him. Through a gap in the trees above, he could see a full moon, brighter than any one he'd ever seen before. It shone down on him from its lofty position, bathing him and the ground around him in silver.

The barn owl suddenly came into view, landing on a tree nearby. Jamie stared as it ruffled its wings. It seemed to gaze down upon him, as if watching over him, as if it knew something he did not; the wise, all-knowing owl.

"What is it that you know, Mr. Owl? What is it you're trying to tell me? Give me your knowledge; give me your wisdom!"

Lauren undressed and stepped into the shower stall, pulling the curtain behind her.

She was quite happy to use this rather than the caravan shower; at least it meant she got away from there. She turned it on and waited till the spray became hot, then got in underneath it.

Her thoughts drifted onto pleasanter things as she stood with the heavy drops massaging her head. She thought of last Friday night, when she'd gone to a friend's house for a party. Guy, her ex with the foul mouth, wasn't there. She'd told him it was over; told him to get a life. Now she was free of him, free to enjoy the party without being embarrassed by something he might say while under the influence.

It was a great party. Sheryl's parents were away for the weekend, so there was plenty of alcohol and cigarettes. They had an amazing music system in their living-room and the walls reverberated to the sound of Pulp and Robbie Williams.

At one stage in the evening, she and Sheryl had taken their drinks up to Sheryl's room and sat on the bed, talking and smoking.

"I can't believe you split up with Guy!"

"He was a jerk! I'm better off without him; if he were here, he would have offended most people by now! You just couldn't trust him not to say anything stupid."

"How are things at home?" asked Sheryl.

"Still the usual shit. Mum and Dad were arguing again the other night. She doesn't stop. Always getting at him; if it's not one thing it's another. She's driving him nuts; she's driving *me* nuts! Sometimes I wish he hadn't married her. She's nothing but an ugly ex-stripper with an alcohol problem!"

Sheryl laughed.

"Here, I've got something that'll cheer you up!"

She leapt off the bed and went to her dressing-table. She went into her underwear drawer and reached into the very back. She returned with a small matchbox-sized re-sealable baggie. Inside were six little tablets.

"Are those what I think they are?" asked Lauren.

"It depends what you think they *are,*" replied Sheryl.

"Where d'you get them?"

"A friend of my brother's; they were dead cheap!"

Lauren took a long drag from her cigarette.

"Give us some ?"

"What did you think I was going to do? Just don't take them here, just in case."

Lauren nodded.

"And don't take more than one at a time, either…"

"Alright, chill out!"

She turned off the shower now, then wrapped herself in her towel. Her jeans were on the floor. She bent down and picked them up, reaching into the pocket for the three pills Sheryl had given her. This was exactly the right time for taking one; she was stressed out. She hadn't actually asked Sheryl what they were, but she knew they were ecstasy. She hoped it would take away the pain. She went over to the basin and turned on the cold tap. She was about to pop it in her mouth, when she stopped. Maybe later, she thought.

At half-past five, the first lot of burgers were ready.

"Grub's up!" announced Bob, waving a pair of pincers.

Lauren was sitting examining a flyer some man had given her on her way back from the shower block. Randolph's Travelling Fair was in town; or in this case, in a large field down the road.

"Dad, d'you want to go to this?" she asked.

"Probably not, sweetheart, I'm a little tired after all that driving. But you go along!"

"What about you, Jamie?" asked Lauren.

Jamie merely nodded as he helped himself to a burger.

The fair was hotching with people. Loud music blasted out from all directions, but the sounds of delighted screaming could not be drowned out. There were stalls galore; shooting galleries, a bouncy castle, a large paddling pool with inflatable globes, a ghost train and lots more besides. Bob had given them both twenty pounds and sent them away.

There was a ride called The Frog, which spun you round and up and down, whilst seated on the end of huge mechanical arms.

"Oh my God, I'm going on that!" shouted Lauren. "You coming?"

Jamie shook his head.

"Suit yourself. Don't spend all your money on sweets, Mum will kill you!"

"Lauren there's…"

But Lauren had already started running towards the ride. It was half past six.

Jamie's shoulders slumped. He looked around him. He didn't feel like going on any rides just now. He spied a van selling slush-puppies and went to buy one. Then he walked off through the crowds, into what seemed like a tunnel of movement and flashing lights. It all seemed blended into one. He was still feeling the anxiety in the pit of his stomach and his surroundings fairly quickly began to make him feel disorientated. Screams from one side; mechanical noises from another.

He had to speak to his sister, whether she would listen to him or not. He had to tell her about mum, about the whisky; it was only fair that she should know. He couldn't keep it a secret. He didn't want to tell his father because he would go ballistic. Something had to be done, but perhaps Lauren would be able to talk her mother out of it, without involving Bob.

He didn't want to go back to the caravan tonight; he wouldn't feel comfortable. This had all happened once before, six years ago. It was his seventh birthday. Perhaps it was the stress of the day, all that organisation. Whatever it was, she got hold of a bottle and locked herself into the bathroom with it.

The strongest image he carried with him from that birthday was that of his father hammering on the outside of the bathroom door and screaming at her. If Bob found that bottle of whisky, it would happen all over again. He couldn't bear that. Just the thought of that image made him want to cry now. Tears welled up in his eyes as he sucked on his icy drink. And everywhere now, he saw people laughing and enjoying themselves, oblivious to the fact that *he* was not.

He brushed away the tears on his cheek and went in search of his sister. He went back to The Frog but the ride had finished and she wasn't there. Where was she? He needed her now. Even though she was his horrible big sister, she was still his sister.

He went to look at the other rides. He examined the queues to see if she was there.

Suddenly he heard his name being called. He looked up. Lauren was strapped into a seat that was slowly ascending some tall structure that looked hellish to any sane person, but to a thrill-seeker like his sister, looked like heaven. "Lauren!" he shouted back. She waved, grinning from ear to ear. "Lauren I need to talk to you!" But his sister was too high up now to hear him. "Lauren!" he shouted, again.

She had reached the top. Suddenly her seat plummeted downwards at colossal speed. He saw her screaming.

Now she was getting out. He would be able to talk to her. But no sooner was she out of her harness than she was off to another ride, running away through the crowd like she was possessed.

"No, wait!" he called.

He ran after her, still shouting. She was heading for the Ghost Train. She paid the attendant and jumped into one of the cars. He wanted to see if he could get in the same car, but somebody got in next to her, and it only held two. Once he'd paid, he got into one as close to her as he could, which was not very close.

The cars started to move. The first one disappeared through the double doors that swung inwards; into the mouth of the skeleton. Its eyes rolled in their sockets and an evil laugh was emitted from some hidden speakers.

Lauren's car disappeared and soon Jamie was also swallowed up. There was an older boy in the seat next to him. As they began going through the 'Caverns of Death', the boy was reaching out and touching the neck of the girl in front, who screamed playfully.

"Cut it out, Connor!"

"What's wrong, I *wasnae* doing anything; it's the *ghosts!*"

"Yea right!" she replied.

"Aye that was the ghosts?" said the boy to Jamie winking at him.

But Jamie was in no mood to play along. He knew his sister was somewhere up ahead, screaming with delight, no doubt. As the ride went on, he began to get more and more anxious. People were screaming all around him; lights flashed in his eyes; grotesque figures loomed towards him out of the semi-darkness. He saw his mother's body lying in her coffin, the empty whisky bottle lying on top of her. Her eyes bulged like the skeleton earlier on and her face was slowly rotting away. Her nails seemed to have shrivelled up, as if they were real all along and her dress was mouldy and seemed to be decaying with age. Jamie screamed now, like everybody else. The boy next to him laughed. "That's right, SCREAM!"

Jamie screamed again, this time with more desperation, and again the boy laughed. "He's loving it!"

But if the lights were any brighter, the boy would have seen Jamie's tears. "Lauren!" he yelled. "Lauren!"

When the ride ended, Jamie leaped out of the car and ran towards his sister.

"Lauren…"

"I don't want to know. Go away!" she shouted. "You didn't have to come if you didn't want to. I'm here to enjoy myself, so don't you dare spoil it!"

"But Lauren, this is *important!"*

"Nothing you say is important, Jamie!"

And with that she was off again. Jamie was sobbing uncontrollably now. Why wouldn't she listen to him? He followed her again. This time she was heading for the dodgems. He followed her onto the ride, but again he couldn't get near her. He found an empty car and got in. They started to move. He could see her on the other side of the ring. He tried to steer towards her, but a car smashed into him from the right and another from the left, jolting him like a rag-doll. He cried even more. Again he tried to steer his way towards his sister.

Lauren saw Jamie now. Why did she have to have such a pathetic little brother?

Couldn't even handle a ghost ride! What was wrong with him? But all the same, something about those tears made her feel guilty about the way she had spoken to him. She turned her car and tried to head in that direction.

"What is it?" she called.

He was yelling something back at her, something about 'Mum'. A car went into the back of Lauren now, and as chance would have it, sent her spinning into her brother's dodgem.

"Jamie, what's the matter?"

"Mum's drinking!" he screamed.

This time she didn't notice the car that came crashing into her; she didn't hear the screams from the other passengers. All she heard was her brother's words ringing in her ears. She stared at his tear-streaked face. Another dodgem collided with her.

Again she hardly noticed. Slowly she turned the wheel and glided away from her brother. But she kept a close eye on him all the same.

It was what she had feared, but still it was a shock to hear it. Could it really have come back to that again? She remembered what it was like before.

As soon as the ride stopped, she was out of her car and walking away. She felt suddenly sick and weak in the legs. She bought a Coke and tipped it down her throat.

Jamie caught up with her. She didn't say anything to him but just kept walking.

"Where are you going?"

"I don't know," she replied.

"Are you going back?"

"I *don't know,*" she reiterated.

There was a little seating area outside a cafe that called itself 'Randolph's Kitchen'. Lauren headed for it. She plonked herself down at a table.

"I think we have to buy something to sit here!" said Jamie.

"Fine, go and get us a large candy floss!"

Jamie went to buy the candy floss; a huge, pink, puffy cloud of melt-in-the-mouth sugar.

Together they sat at that table and picked bits off the floss between them. Neither of them said anything for a while. Jamie didn't know what to say, if anything at all. Lauren couldn't really get her head around the bad news.

"Do you remember your seventh birthday?" she asked, suddenly.

Jamie nodded.

"I was thinking about that earlier," he replied.

"What do you remember of it?"

"I remember it was the worst day of my life!" he said. "Up till now."

Lauren popped more candy floss into her mouth.

"Shall I tell you what I remember of it?"

Jamie shrugged in a non-committal way.

"I remember I was cleaning plates and food away when I heard Dad shouting. Mum had gone out to the shop, twenty minutes earlier. She said she was going to get more Smarties, but she didn't; she bought a bottle of vodka. And she brought that bottle of vodka home, went upstairs and locked herself in the bathroom with it. Dad must have known what she was up to.

I left the plates and went up to see what was going on. I saw Dad standing outside the bathroom; he was banging on the door.

"Elaine! For God's sake, what are you doing?"
"Go away!" she screamed back. "It's none of your business!"
"Have you got a bottle in there? Have you? Is that what's going on?"

"Mum was crying. I could hear her," said Lauren to Jamie.

"I can't do it anymore!" she shouted.
"Yea, you bloody can! You can do it for me, and you can do it for the kids!"
"No, I can't!" she wailed.
"Then you'll have to go back into rehab, and what am I going to do then? How am I going to cope?"

Lauren continued, "I saw you, right then; sitting in your bedroom doorway, watching all of it. I felt so sorry for you, Jamie. It was your birthday. Mum had bought you that football, remember? Jamie nodded.

"You don't need me!" said Elaine. "I'm a burden to you; you hate me! You wish you'd never married me!"

21

"You're talking rubbish, Elaine. I love you; you're the love of my life! I can't do without you! Please come out. Come out and talk to me!"

"She did come out," Lauren continued. "It took her a few minutes, right enough, but she did open that door. She flopped into Dad's arms, remember?"

"I remember. They sank down onto the floor together. They held each other for a long time, crying."

"For God sake, Elaine, don't ever bloody do that again! You know what the doctor said. I don't know what I'd do if I lost you!"

"I could see you crying, too," said Jamie. "I could also see my friends on the stairs behind you. They were watching, as well." Jamie began to cry again. "It was my birthday. It was supposed to be a happy day. I was looking forward to it for ages."

Lauren's chin quivered as she looked across at her little brother.

"Why did it happen on *my* birthday? Does nobody in this family want me?"

He put his arms on the table and buried his face in them. Lauren also began to cry now.

The two of them sat sobbing at that table, while all around them, the fair was in full swing.

"Of course we want you, Jamie!"

But Jamie didn't let up his tears. Lauren reached across the table and touched her brother's arm.

"Please!" she said.

Jamie pushed her hand away. Lauren waited for him to calm down a little.

"I remember the arguments as well," he said. "I could hear them through the floor of my room sometimes, when I was lying in bed at night. I used to get scared. I could hear my name being mentioned, but I couldn't hear what they were saying. I heard so many arguments about me that I started to realise that I was the problem. That's why Dad was always shouting at me. He never shouted at you; he never ridiculed you; he never called you a pain in the arse and told you to shut up. And why, because he hates me and wishes I was never born! Do you know what I think all those conversations were about; they were about wanting to re-house me; they wanted to get rid of me, send me to another family!"

"No, Jamie, that's not *true.*"

"It *is* true! Why are you always mean to me? Why did you never once stand up for me? Did you not ever stop to think that maybe I, your little brother, might have wanted your help?"

"I'm sorry!" sobbed Lauren. "I'm really sorry!"

"No you're not!"

"Jamie, listen to me, I'm just a *cow!* I didn't mean all the things I said! I love you, Jamie! You're the best thing in my flaming life! You're not an alcoholic and you're not a fat slob; you're *perfect.* Do you not understand, Jamie; everything I say, I say it because I'm angry with the situation! I'm not angry with you! I'm angry because I live in that *shithole* with parents who can't even get on with each other! With a mother who's one swig away from dying, and a father whose only real interests in life are Manchester City Football Club and building caravans. Whoopee! What a wonderful great load of prospects I've got!"

Jamie dried his eyes.

"But Jamie, I've got to tell you something now. You're not going to like it, but I have to tell you."

"What is it?" he asked.

Lauren put a hand over her mouth. She took a deep breath.

"Jamie, I know the reason Dad's always shouting at you. I know the reason they were having those arguments about you."

"What reason is that?"

"Because…"

She stopped.

"Because, what?" prompted her brother.

She shook her head.

"No, I can't. I can't tell you, forget I said it!"

"I'm not forgetting it, Lauren. What is it? What's the reason?"

"Because Mum had an *affair!*" she screamed.

Jamie stared at his sister.

"What?"

Lauren nodded, slowly.

"Because of Mum's drinking, the two of them were having problems with each other. Mum had an affair with one of her clients. She got pregnant. The man split and ran off. When Dad found out, he went mental. He told me all this when I was old enough to understand. He threatened to divorce her and take me with him. But eventually he changed his mind. Bob's not your real dad, Jamie!"

Jamie sat very still. He looked confused; he wiped away a stray tear from his cheek.

"I'm…I'm the result of an affair?" he asked, slowly. "I'm an accident…"

"No, Jamie, you're no accident, don't even think that."

"But...Mum's boyfriend wasn't interested; Mum didn't really want to have me and Dad or *Bob,* or whoever he is, sure as *shit* doesn't want me. And that's because I'm a permanent reminder of the affair his wife had!" He looked at his sister, his eyes brimming with tears again. "That just leaves you."

Lauren said nothing; she stared back at her brother, with an expression full of woe.

"Do *you* want me?"

"Of course I want you, Jamie; I've said that."

Jamie stared hard at her for several seconds.

"I don't believe you!"

And with that he pushed back his chair and ran from the cafe.

"Jamie come back!" shouted Lauren.

But he wasn't listening and he wasn't going to stop. He ran from the fun fair and back along the road to Forest Brae. But he didn't go near the caravan, instead he ran in the opposite direction. He ran until he almost doubled up and collapsed with exhaustion.

He hadn't been aware of where he was going, since it didn't matter to him. But now, as he paused for breath, he realised he didn't recognise this area of the campsite.

He straightened up and looked around him. He seemed to have run into a patch of forest, and yet it was still landscaped. They'd obviously extended the site since he'd last visited.

He began to walk now. The trees were tall here, and one or two Scots pines partially obscured the sunlight. The plots here were tucked away from the main body of the campsite, and were perhaps more exclusive than the others. He spotted a chalet with beautiful decking and hanging baskets.

He had been wandering along looking at these new plots, and had just decided to turn back, when he saw it.

It was just a fleeting glimpse to begin with, a suggestion of bright colours through the foliage.

He followed the path round so he could get a better look. It was the last plot. But this one did not contain a flashy, modern motor home. What it contained was something quite different. Something Jamie had only seen in photographs but never for real.

In the centre of a little clearing, nicely tucked away from prying eyes, was a very old, but very beautiful, gypsy caravan.

Chapter Two

The Gypsy

Jamie stared for a long time. Eventually he walked slowly towards it. A cart-horse was grazing on the short grass, over to his right. It didn't even look up. The caravan had a pale green canvas roof, with a little chimney pipe smoking peacefully away. The exterior was predominantly yellow, with red outlines of horses painted in a border around the side. Stencilled flowers adorned the front door, above which were two little windows that were now standing open, as if to let in the evening breeze. Wind chimes hung down from the canopy on either side, producing a gentle and mystical sound, which at that moment was the only thing Jamie could hear.

He was almost bewitched. It was such a magical scene that had suddenly sprung up before him, like a painting, but far better. He was really there, taking it all in; watching the horse happily munching, listening to the wind chimes. He moved further into the painting, and became a part of it. The boy, the caravan, the horse; it was all one image.

And it was then, at that surreal moment, that the gypsy appeared. He emerged from the interior, gently pushing open the door and stepping out.

The boy and he observed each other. Neither spoke. The chimes whistled a little louder as the breeze suddenly increased and the rim of the gypsy's hat flapped up for a moment. A white beard surrounded a pair of dry lips, and the dappled sunlight danced across his rugged features.

Their eyes met now; and it was in that instant that something of what; recognition, could it be, flashed between them. He had never seen this man in his life, but at the same time Jamie almost could have sworn that he had. Either that or he reminded him of someone else.

"Good evening," said the gypsy, at last.

"Good evening," Jamie found himself replying.

He still stared.

"Do you like her?" asked the gypsy.

"Her?" enquired Jamie.

The gypsy indicated to the caravan. Jamie nodded.

"It's beautiful. Is it yours?"

"Oh yes," replied the gypsy, nodding, "very much mine. And my mother's before me. She came down through the family."

"Why do you call it her?" asked Jamie.

"It gives her a personality; which she definitely has. Everything has a personality, not just us. Mojo, my horse, the birds, the trees, the flowers; even the grass you're standing on."

Jamie raised his eyebrows.

"The grass has a personality, does it?" he said, sceptically.

"Of course. It's wild, grows at its own pace and has its own unique smell."

The gypsy descended the little wooden steps and came towards him. He extended a rough hand.

"Moses!" he said, by way of introduction.

Jamie shook it in return and gave his own name.

"Nice to meet you," said Moses.

His voice, Jamie found, was very hypnotic. His tone was not gruff, but rather, smooth.

He thought suddenly that if one could see a person's tone, Moses' would resemble the gas emitted from a fine bottle of champagne just after it was opened. His accent was a curious mix of foreign and English, but the two seemed to have gelled seamlessly together.

"Where are you from?" asked Jamie.

"Originally from Czechoslovakia, what you now call the Czech Republic. But we travelled a lot as gypsies will do."

He smiled.

"What brings you here?" asked Jamie.

"I love Scotland. I come every year and stay in different places. Mojo over there has served me well." He looked at him now, his nose right down to the ground. "Poor old fellow; I think he prefers *long* grass." Moses chuckled. "And what about yourself; what are your origins?"

"Manchester."

"Ah, you're a city boy. Do you like it there?"

"No, I'd rather be almost anywhere else."

Moses nodded.

"You sound a bit English yourself," said Jamie.

"I came to England nearly twenty years ago and settled for a time in Dorset. I stayed with a little community of gypsies there."

"I'd like to travel," said Jamie. "See the rest of the world. See how other people live."

Moses observed him for a few moments in silence.

"Well," he said, suddenly, "I was just about to put a kettle on the burner. Would you like to join me?"

Jamie smiled.

"Can I?" he asked, sheepishly.

"Of course. We can sit outside since it's a pleasant evening, that is, if the midgies aren't around!"

Moses went back to the caravan. On the left, just inside the door, was a small, wood burning stove.

"Come in if you like, have a look at her."

Jamie walked up the steps and peered in. It was the cosiest, neatest little place he'd ever seen. At the far end of the caravan was a compact, snug-looking bunk, with a little round window above it. A long settle was the main feature on the right-hand side, with a fold-away table in front of it. Opposite that was what looked like a dressing-table, crammed with lots of different things; a photo in a frame, a carved wooden box, a pack of cigars and a pipe, a deck of cards, a watercolour of an impressive-looking building and so on.

There were drawers underneath, and other watercolours on the walls, along with a shelf containing crockery. Moses opened a small fridge and took out some milk.

"I'm afraid there's not much I can offer you, except tea or apple juice."

"Could I have apple juice, please?" asked Jamie, rather politely.

"Apple juice it is then," said Moses.

Jamie was looking at the photo in the frame. It was an old, black and white image of a young gypsy woman. Her hair was under a pale scarf; her skin had a dark complexion. Beads hung around her neck, while from her ears, hung what looked like handmade earrings. She was staring at the camera, her features strong and bold; her gaze, powerful and unflinching.

"That's my mother," said Moses, pouring tea into a mug.

"She's very pretty," remarked Jamie.

"She was quite a character in her day."

They took the drinks out to the front steps and sat down.

"It was she who thought of the name Moses. Do you know the story of Moses?"

"Yes; we did it in religious studies."

"Whilst still in labour with me, my mother decided to wash clothes at the same time. It was, I believe, quite a long labour, and my mother was not the sort of person who just sat around. We were staying in a little camp on the banks of the Voltava. The story goes that as she was rinsing a pair of socks in the shallows, I arrived. As soon as she had delivered me, she put me straight in the washing basket. Hence my name."

Moses smiled. Jamie sipped on his apple juice.

"If you moved around a lot, where did you go to school?"

"My *mother* was my school. She taught me everything I needed to know, initially. While I was in Dorset, I enrolled in a local college and got my basic qualifications. After that I went on to study History of Art at the same college. In the community was an artist who painted with watercolours. His paintings were so beautiful that I asked him to teach me. It was he who suggested the History of Art course. Now I paint for a living and I travel around and sell them. The ones inside are all mine."

Jamie stared at the trees for a while. Moses blew on his tea.

"And what about your father?" asked Jamie, rather quietly.

"My father died when I was very young, so I never knew him."

Jamie nodded, slowly. He thought about Bob, the man who wasn't his dad, the man who resented him.

"Did you like your Mum?" he asked.

"Very much. We were very close. She was all I had. And I was all *she* had. We looked after each other. I kept her company through the long years without him, and I grew to know her very well as a person. My mother was very spiritual; something she had inherited from *her* mother." Moses swirled his tea and took a sip. "My mother was what you call a 'seer'; that means someone with second sight; a 'sensitive'. She had the ability to see beyond the 'veil', as we call it. She read palms, tarot cards; she even read tea leaves from time to time. She could tell you if your baby would be a boy or a girl." Again, Moses took a sip of tea. "She could also communicate, so she claimed, with people no longer living."

Jamie stared at Moses. A slight shiver ran down through his body. The wind chimes howled.

"How did she do that?" asked Jamie.

"She just had the ability."

"Do you?" he asked.

Moses smiled and shook his head.

"No. At least, I don't think I do. To tell you the truth I've never tried."

"Didn't it ever scare you?"

"No." Moses laid his mug down on the step. He turned more towards Jamie now as he spoke. "You see my mother was not only good at mediumship, she was also a very talented storyteller. A large part of my education was communicated to me through stories. She explained to me that storytelling was the oldest form of communication around; it's how our ancestors communicated and how we learned about them; by telling stories and passing them on down through the generations. Folklore, fairy tales, ghost stories; they were all told round the fire. Gypsies are very good storytellers, and my mother was one of them. She learned the art from my grandfather, who used to tell my mother stories all the time."

"Stories about what?" asked Jamie.

"Mostly about the spirit world; the world that we all come from, and the world that we return to when we die."

Jamie felt his face go warm suddenly. Hot little prickles began to seep out from under the skin. He felt the tears coming back.

"Are you alright?" asked Moses, when he noticed the boy's change in behaviour.

Jamie could not stop the tears from returning. His chest heaved and he began to cry in front of this stranger.

Moses put a gentle hand on his back. He slowly began to rub it, very gently, in a circular motion.

"It's okay, Jamie," he said, quietly. "Let it out; let out whatever's bottled up inside that head of yours."

Jamie sobbed bitterly. He couldn't help it. He didn't care anymore.

"I wish I was dead. There's nothing here for me; nobody who wants me. I'm the son of a pervert! The son of the man who had an affair with my mum and then abandoned her! Her husband, the man I thought was my dad, hates me, and he wishes I'd never been born. So do I! I am nothing. I belong to nobody. I am a mistake, something that shouldn't have happened. I was not planned for!"

Jamie's nose was running, and he dribbled like a baby. Moses just listened, his hand still rubbing the boy's back. "I always felt like I'd been born into the wrong family. And now I know it's true. My sister is not my sister, and my dad is not my dad. The only person I really belong to is my mum, and she doesn't even want to know. Why? It wasn't my fault she had an affair. It was her own! *She's* the alcoholic, not me, and she's the one who wants to kill herself! Why are they taking it out on me?"

He cried for another ten minutes before calming down and drying his eyes. Moses gave him a hanky to wipe his nose.

"I'm so sorry!" said Moses, gently. "That's horrible."

"It's okay," replied, Jamie. "I'm sorry I cried in front of you."

Moses' already creased brow began to crease even more.

"It's alright for boys to cry in front of men, Jamie, you needn't apologise. Surely you've cried in front of your... stepfather before?"

"Only once, and he called me a pansy!"

Moses shook his head.

"I saw my sister cry once. She'd been reading a newspaper article about starving children in Ethiopia. Apparently it had really affected her. She actually gave me a hug; I don't know why."

"Well if it makes you feel any better, I cried just the other night there."

Jamie looked at him sheepishly.

"What were *you* crying for?"

"Oh I was reading a novel."

"Which was?"

"*Black Beauty*! Have you heard of it?"

Jamie let out a snigger.

"What?" exclaimed Moses. "It's a very emotional book, I'll have you know. I have a particular soft spot for horses!"

Jamie laughed. Then he stopped and sighed.

"You're just winding me up," he said.

"No," said Moses, "just trying to make you smile. And it worked. Another apple juice, young sir?"

Jamie nodded. Moses rose and fetched him more.

"Anyway, I was about to say earlier on that a lot of the stories my mother told me were about spirits and spiritualism, and each one had a particular lesson to it. But they were all positive stories, not negative in any way, and always entertaining. So I never feared what my mother did, because I understood it. Do you see?"

Jamie nodded.

"And can *you* tell stories?"

"Yes," replied Moses, "I can."

"My mum hardly ever read me a bedtime story. When she did, it was only because I begged her, and then she would always say, *'Okay, but just a short one and then you go to sleep.'* I don't think she liked reading to me very much. She's not very motherly, my mum."

"Do *you* read much?" asked Moses.

"A little. We don't have many books in the house, and the nearest library is about forty-five minutes away from our part of town."

"What type of stories interest you and capture your imagination?"

"Adventure stories; fairy tales, that sort of thing. I liked Peter Pan. Things that…"

Jamie paused, to think of the word. "…*distract* you from…this world. That's why I would read a book."

Moses nodded.

"And that's a very good reason, too. Most people read because it takes them out of themselves for a time. But it depends what you read, I suppose. There are books that are there simply to entertain, while others teach you a particular moral or lesson. And some are factual; they tell you about the world. Then there are other stories that blend all that together in one. But listening to someone *tell* you a story is a very different experience to actually reading it yourself. It's nice to be told a story, and that's why it's very important when our parents tell us stories before bed. They fire our imaginations before we dream; it's something to look forward to at the end of a school day. And it's about bonding as well, the bond between parent and child. That's why I think parents who don't read their children bedtime stories are missing an opportunity."

Jamie looked at him very steadily. Moses continued to drink his tea. He looked over at Mojo, who was still busy eating.

"What about painting?" asked Jamie. "That's creating as well."

"Absolutely; and it's interesting you bring that up because there are similarities. A painting tells a story, sets a scene or creates a certain mood in the viewer. But that is of course very much visual, no words, so it's a different type of medium, but it can still have the same sort of effect on someone. If you buy a painting and put it on your wall, it's because that painting speaks to you. And that's why some books, especially children's books, have drawings in them, because that adds another dimension to the story."

Jamie nodded and began to speak, "I remember one of my favourite stories had really nice drawings in it. I got my mum to buy it for me when I was little. It was a story about a barn owl. The drawings were…peaceful, if you know what I mean? The owl lived in this lovely wood in a big, old oak tree. And from where he sat, he could see out over the treetops towards the fields, where Farmer Brown would be out feeding his sheep. It was the way the drawings were done; everything looked perfect and soft; there were always fluffy clouds in the sky; the fields were all green and lush; the sheep looked happy. It was comforting."

Moses nodded, slowly, a broad smile on his face.

"That's how it should be. And you remember that, you see; it's a nice memory from your early childhood."

"And now I've got the rest of teenage-hood to look forward to. What fun!"

"Maybe it *will* be fun, you don't know. Things change, Jamie; you don't think it, but they do. Childhood is very different from the rest of your life."

"But doesn't what happens to you in childhood *affect* the rest of your life?"

"Not if you don't let it. You can choose to move on."

Jamie looked away.

"That's easy for you to say, Moses. You haven't been through what I've been through."

"True. But I've been through different things that were just as taxing."

Jamie picked his nails.

"What have you been through?" he asked, quietly.

"The worst thing I went through was abuse at the hands of locals. Verbal and sometimes physical. Wherever we went it seemed, there was always somebody who didn't want us there. Boys my age, who lived 'normal lives' as they called it, would treat me as an outsider. Because we had no fixed abode, I couldn't go to school. One of the camps we were at was in a field. Boys used to come and stand on the gate and shout things at us. We had several caravans burned and people were beaten up, including myself. We left that place fairly quickly."

"What happened?" asked Jamie.

"I was out for a walk late one evening, against my mum's wishes; she knew how dangerous it was. I was set upon by five youths; thrown to the ground, kicked, punched. It only stopped when a group of other gypsies intervened. They gave those boys a licking they wouldn't forget in a hurry. We packed up that night and moved on before the police got involved."

Jamie was still picking his nails.

"I remember one evening, getting ready for bed. It was a Friday. My fath... Bob came in."

"I told you to put your school clothes in the washing basket, didn't I?"

"Oh!"

"Oh! Is that all you have to say, you lazy little bugger? Get downstairs and put them in now!"

"I did as I was told," said Jamie to Moses. "He came down with me."

"I've got football to watch at eight, I wanted to get this out of the way and done by now!"

"You've still got five minutes!"

"I beg your pardon?"

"I said you've still got..."

"Suddenly he grabbed my head and shoved it into the washing machine!"

"You cheeky little bastard! I'll wash your mouth out with flaming detergent! Don't you ever speak to me like that again! You start pulling your weight around this house more than you do, young man! Don't make the mistake of thinking I love you, Jamie. You got that? Never!"

"And with that, he pulled my head out of the machine before slamming the door and turning it on. Then he marched off to watch his *frigging* football!" Jamie's fists were clenching. "The next day I went to the school psychologist. It wasn't the last time he was violent with me."

*   *   *   *

Lauren stared at the screen in front of her. This time it was a large games console she was playing in the arcade, and not her mobile phone. Her expression was blank, as she fought her way through a Jurassic landscape of man-eating dinosaurs. It was nine o'clock. When the game was over, she wandered away from it and headed for the cafe. She bought a Coke and sat down at one of the tables. There weren't many people around. The cafe was cheaply decorated with plastic tables and chairs and bright colours. They were probably supposed to make people feel happy, but it was so bland that it was depressing.

It certainly did not improve her mood just now. Depressed didn't really cover it. It seemed to go deeper than that; almost to despair. At that moment as she sat at the table, she had no compulsion to move or hardly even to drink her large, Coke syrup mixture that cost her three pounds.

Her thoughts were on her brother. She hadn't seen him since he'd run off. He hadn't gone back to the caravan, according to her mother. She thought he might be here, that's why she came, but he wasn't here either. He obviously needed to be on his own, and it was probably best just to leave him be if that was the case. To suddenly discover that your family life was a lie, must hit anybody hard. 'Poor boy,' she thought, 'he's been treated like shit all his life, and now he discovers the reason for that is because he was, as he put it, *an accident.*' But she didn't want him to think like that; it was not fair. She had been as horrible to him as everybody else; but she hadn't meant to be.

Jamie was the sunlight in their family; the outsider that had brought illumination into the dark circle. He was the innocent one. Not that she wasn't innocent herself. She had suffered too with her mother's behaviour.

Jamie was right; *why* couldn't she have been nice to him? Why couldn't she have taken him under her wing and sheltered him from the horrors that she had gone through? Because she wasn't strong enough, that's why. Jamie was the strong one; *he* had the strength in the family.

She sucked up syrup through her straw. She remembered when Jamie was born. She had gone with Bob to the hospital to see him. Bob was not there for the delivery; he'd been working. Lauren was at nursery. Elaine had got herself to the hospital in a taxi after going into labour. She'd phoned Bob about halfway through. Her mother had told her later that he had refused to attend. Even aged three, she had vague memories of the agro and upset following this momentous occasion. She remembered sitting in front of the gas fire in the living-room and watching her parents shout at each other, as though she hadn't been in the room. She had wondered what it was all about.

She remembered a bathtime once with baby Jamie. It was Bob who had been given the task of washing him and putting him into his night clothes. Again he had seemed very angry when doing this. She saw his rough treatment of her brother, which had caused him to cry. A brief scrub with the soap; a splash or two of water, the manhandling as he dumped little Jamie down on the bathmat and shoved him into his cotton bodysuit.

"What's wrong?" she had asked.

Bob had replied, "Daddy can't be arsed!"

Lauren suddenly stopped sucking on her straw. A horrible thought had just occurred to her. The bruises Jamie had sustained in one or two rugby matches. My God! Both times, Bob had gone to pick him up from games. Jamie wasn't a big fan of rugby; he wasn't in the scrum and he never liked to get his hands on the ball, in case he was tackled. So why had he ended up with such extensive bruising, especially around the face? She now put two and two together and got a twisted four. If her father had mistreated Jamie at the tender age of three months; what was the likelihood he would do it again, when older? It was a high likelihood. And especially as Lauren now knew why.

She left the cafe and went to the toilets. She splashed water on her face and sobbed.

"I'm sorry, Jamie!" she said, to her reflection in the mirror. "I'm so sorry. I should have realised earlier. I should have stood up for you. You have every right to hate me, too!"

She locked herself in a cubicle and, trembling all over, removed the baggie from her pocket. She stared at the pills but could not bring herself to swallow them. She slumped onto the floor in front of the basins and continued to cry. She had failed her half-brother, who was just as vulnerable as she was. She had not seen, nor had she read between the lines.

Images and memories flashed through her mind. She remembered listening to her parents arguing downstairs one night. She had been trying to get to sleep. The light was off, but that was okay, there was always streetlight that came in through the flimsy, white curtains. She felt peaceful, watching the car lights illuminating her wall as they came down the road. It had a hypnotic and soothing effect on Lauren, for whatever reason.

And then she heard her father's raised voice from downstairs. Her stomach immediately tightened. She felt nervous tingles all over her body. She tensed every muscle. She never heard all of the argument, just snippets of it; the loudest bits.

"Look at yourself! Call yourself a mother? You're nothing but a slut!"

And then a plate smashed. Lauren threw back her covers and leapt out. She scuttled under her bed, where she often played, and where her My Little Pony was now waiting for her. Her mother had bought it for her in a charity shop one day, saying that she remembered that from her childhood. It was pink with a yellow mane. She called it Akina. She loved it. She'd made a stable for it under her bed, and would get grass from the garden, to feed it. Now she clutched it tightly to her, as the row went on downstairs.

"Did you get bored of me, was that it?"

"I wasn't bored; I was angry! You're the one who stopped speaking to me, so what was I supposed to think?"

And then a few minutes later…

"I had to quit my job! I loved it, but I had to quit. Eighty pounds a week, that's all I got! Nappies, bed time, meal times! And all because you couldn't handle your drink!"

A glass smashed.

"Stop it!"

"Was he good, was he? Did he make you feel special? I hope he was worth it! Because now every time I look at Jamie, I'm reminded of him! I can also see him!"

"What d'you mean?"

"Well, Jamie has none of my traits and he has none of yours either; so he must look like that bastard!"

Back then, Lauren had no idea really what they were arguing about, except that her brother was somehow involved. Maybe that was why she was mean to Jamie? He had upset her daddy as well, not just her mother.

Another image flashed into her mind.

She was twelve; her friends were round at her house; her parents were out. They had decided to tease Jamie. He was in his room, probably talking to himself, the weirdo. They snuck up to his door, Lauren in front. She popped it open. Jamie was sitting at his little desk, his back to them.

"Hey, weirdo, my friends have come to have a look at you!"

They all laughed.

"What are you doing?"

"None of your business!"

Lauren marched into the room. She peered over his shoulder.

"He's drawing something!"

"Go away!" he shouted.

"It looks like he's attempting to draw a bird. The only reason I can tell it's a bird is because it's sitting in what is obviously a tree. I wouldn't be able to tell otherwise."

There was a huge bruise on the right side of his face.

43

"Did you get into a fight?"

"Rugby!" he said.

"Rugby? How would you get a bruise like that playing rugby? You're crap! You don't go anywhere near the ball and you don't go in for tackles!"

"Get out of my room!" he screamed, standing up now.

"With pleasure!"

She left.

"What a pathetic brother you've got!" said one of her friends.

More laughter.

"I'm sorry, Jamie," she whispered. "I'm so sorry!"

She remembered then, an odd incident; odd because of the way she had responded to it.

One of the rare times she had actually felt affection for her brother was in a play park about ten minutes from their house. There was a big sandpit for children to play in. Jamie was jumping around in it excitedly. They were there with Elaine. There was no danger in that sandpit and it was a safe environment. And yet all of a sudden, as she watched her brother rolling around in the sand, a sense of extreme fear came over her.

She didn't want him in there anymore; she wanted to drag him out, put her arms around him and never let go. And that's what she did. Jamie protested a little, but then seemed to accept the embrace. Elaine wondered what she was doing, but she said nothing.

What had prompted her to feel that way? That same night, Lauren had a very disturbing dream.

She was in a hot country, in a small village with ramshackle houses. All about them was desert. The sun was unbearably hot, even in the shade. She was weak from hunger. As she walked, she knew she was looking for somebody. She was worried about this person.

Suddenly, as she rounded the corner of a house, she saw a small boy lying face down in the sand; his little body, frail and horrifyingly thin. It was Jamie. She ran forward, screaming out his name. He didn't move. He couldn't move; he had been dead for several hours. Flies had begun to congregate and in a nearby tree sat two vultures.

Lauren had woken with a start and immediately begun to cry. She had gone through to her brother's room, where he was sleeping peacefully and kissed her baby sibling.

She had experienced that dream several more times over the period of a year, before it had disappeared from her mind.

She now thought about the strangeness of it. She had not thought about that dream for years. What had it meant? Was she afraid of losing him? She didn't *like* him! Maybe that's why the memory of it had come back now. Jamie was missing. She wanted to find him, she wanted, again, to put her arms around him and never let him go.

She heard the bathroom door open and somebody came in. They went into the adjacent cubicle. She suddenly heard the woman begin to talk to herself.

"Mum? Is that you?"

"Lauren?"

"What are you doing here?"

"Havin' a pee."

Lauren rolled her eyes.

"I mean, why are you in the gaming arcade?"

"I was looking for Jamie."

Lauren scoffed.

"Really. And what do *you* care about him?"

"Come again?"

"You heard me. Since when have you been worried about Jamie? Since when have *any* of us been worried about him?"

"I don't know what you're talking about, I'm his *mother,* for Christ sake; of course I'm worried about him!"

"Come off it! I don't think you've worried about any of us for a long time. I think you're just worried about yourself!"

Elaine was silent. Lauren was glad there was a partition between them.

"Jamie told me he saw you buying whisky…"

"What?"

"Yea! He saw you, and it upset him no end. And d'you know what? He was worried about *you!* He was worried about you dying!"

"Oh God!" she heard her mother whisper.

"Is that what this is all about; killing yourself? Leaving us two with that fat ignoramus…"

"Don't talk about your father like that!"

"Oh what would you like me to say; he's a prince with endless wealth, as well as endless kindness? Did you know he's hit Jamie before?"

This time there was a longer silence from the next door cubicle.

"Don't you dare tell me you knew?"

"Well *you* obviously do!"

"I've just bloody well worked it out! You *did* know, didn't you? And for how long?"

She didn't respond. Lauren banged on the cubicle wall.

"Answer me!" she yelled.

Her mother sighed.

"Ever since I saw the first bruise."

"You *bitch!*" hissed Lauren. "What, couldn't you confront Dad? Were you afraid he would hit you too?"

"Yes," responded her mother, after a pause. "Okay, I was afraid he would hit me. I mean, what if I was wrong?"

"You could have asked Jamie? He's your son after all, I thought you were worried about him?"

She heard her mother sniffling.

"The truth is that you didn't have the *bottle* to do anything. You didn't want it to be true. You wanted to bury your head in the sand and try and pretend it was a happy family you were living in. But it's never been a happy family, Mum."

Elaine sat on the toilet with the handbag at her feet. She stared at the tiles, a tear trickling down her nose.

"Never?" she asked, quietly.

"Never!" repeated Lauren.

Elaine sniffed. "I'm sorry," she said.

In her hand, she held the whisky bottle. She held it carefully, lovingly; gently caressing the cold, smooth glass. She gazed at the brown substance inside.

"Why don't you do it, then?" came her daughter's voice, as though she could see her through the wall.

"Do what?"

"Drink it! It's what you want, isn't it? To kill yourself. So why not; nobody wants you, least of all me!"

Lauren's fists were clenched, her face screwed into an expression of loathing.

"But before you die, remember the legacy you'll leave behind: two messed-up children who have no life now."

Elaine burst into tears.

"I know, I know! You think I'm proud of it? My entire life has been nothing but hell! I've had no life from the age of thirteen because I've been an alcoholic. I hoped I could give my children…something better!"

"Oh you really did *that,* didn't you!" said Lauren, sarcastically.

"I'm sorry. I'm sorry for being a terrible mother. I'm sorry for ruining your life. I'm sorry I didn't protect Jamie. Jesus, I'm sorry for everything! If I could go back and do it all again, I would have stayed away from those drinking sessions in the park…"

"But you can't, Mum, you can't turn back time. What's done is done, and don't you ever forget it!"

Elaine sobbed. Lauren sat with her head against the tiled wall and closed her eyes. If she took the pills, all this pain would go away, and she would be able to cope again. Let her mother drink that whisky, let her destroy her insides; what did *she* care. Her only other wish was that it would be slow and painful.

But what she had said before was right. She had no life now, just as her brother had no life. If her mother died, she would leave home. She didn't want to be with her father anymore, not after this knowledge. The only person she cared about now was Jamie. There would be no more teasing, shouting at him or putting him down. All of that ended from today.

Elaine cried for a full fifteen minutes. Her daughter said nothing more to her. She didn't deserve two such beautiful children as Lauren and Jamie. She had done nothing for them. She remembered a trip to the beach once, when they were little, and seeing all the other families with their little children, happily playing in the sand or swimming in the sea. Even back then, she had felt something was missing in her relationship with her own children. It all seemed so cheery, but there was no cheeriness with her. She knew the disdain Bob had for Jamie, and even *she* harboured feelings of guilt and resentment, which seemed to have morphed into the neglect of her son.

She unscrewed the bottle and raised it to her nose, breathing in that glorious smell. The fumes rushed up into her brain and reminded her of the joy drinking had once given her. She recalled all the old sensations. She put the bottle to her lips. She paused and her life flashed before her. She saw Jamie in his late teens, about to graduate from school. She saw Lauren with a baby and husband. She saw Bob as the proud grandparent, carrying his little grandson around in a tiny Manchester City top. Was it possible, or just wishful thinking? The bottle was still tilted to her lips.

Lauren left the cubicle. "Don't bloody follow me!" she shouted, and banged the door behind her. She needed to blow off steam. She headed back to the caravan. Bob was sitting outside; a can of beer in one hand and a cigarette in the other. She ignored him and went inside. She retrieved her jogging gear and headed for the gym.

*　　*　　*　　*

Jamie took a deep breath.

"He came to pick me up from rugby one afternoon. I had been on the sidelines the whole time. I got into the front seat and belted up. We drove in the usual direction for a time, until Bob turned off the road and drove down a small side street. Here he parked the car, and then just sat in silence for a while. He didn't look at me, just stared out the front windscreen as if something was on his mind. I didn't trust myself to speak.

Suddenly he turned his face and looked at me. There was a completely blank expression on his face; no emotion. I remember asking him if he was okay.

Without even answering, he punched me on the side of my head. It was hard. And then he went ballistic. He grabbed me and slammed my face against the side window, punching and slapping me at the same time. Throughout this he made no sound at all.

The attack lasted maybe only thirty seconds but it felt far longer. My lip and my nose were bleeding by the time it was over. I was too shocked to do or say anything. As for Bob, he simply turned the engine back on and carried on driving. That happened twice!"

Jamie removed his inhaler from his pocket and breathed in a puff of gas. He jostled his knee, a sign of tension. He closed his eyes. He felt the panic attack returning.

He saw his owl; calm and serene, sitting on its branch. It winked at him.

"What are you trying to tell me, Mr. Owl?"

He heard its call.

Moses touched him gently on his arm. He opened his eyes.

"All right?" he asked.

Jamie shrugged.

Moses went back into the caravan and started making himself another cup of tea.

Jamie followed him and sat looking at one of his paintings. Moses was quiet for a time, almost pensive. Once or twice he glanced over at Jamie, who seemed not to notice. Moses added a teabag to the boiling water and let it brew. There was silence; even the wind chimes seemed to have stopped.

"Jamie?"

The boy looked up at him.

"What are you thinking just now?"

"I was thinking about that picture, there, the one of the waterfall. I was thinking what you were saying about it telling a story."

"Would you like to hear one?" asked Moses, quietly.

Jamie nodded.

"Yes, I would. Can you tell me it now?"

Chapter Three

The Story Begins

Prince Corliss stood, gazing down into the mist. From where he stood on the clifftop, he could see, rising out of that perfect white vapour, the stunning marble turrets of his father's palace. Beyond that he could see the majestic mountains to the north of the great city of Edomite, the capital of his father's kingdom, Amal, a place he had called home for almost twenty-one years. The Kingdom of Amal was hemmed on all sides by an awesome collection of mountain ranges, with their caps as sharp as spikes and their glaciers glistening in the sun.

Prince Corliss narrowed his eyes. Beyond the kingdom, lay another world. A world he had never ventured into, a world of fear and danger. Within his father's kingdom there was no fear, only happiness, and a feeling of immense peace. There was nothing that induced him to journey beyond it. The North Gate of the great city, Edomite's 'backdoor', opened right out into The Land Beyond, as it was known. It was heavily guarded by a hundred men.

Corliss wiped sweat from his troubled brow. In exactly two months from today, he would be turning twenty-one; and that meant one thing: he would have to leave the kingdom to venture into The Land Beyond. It was a matter of course and an ancient tradition. When the prince of the realm reached his twenty-first birthday, he must marry and leave with his princess to experience a life elsewhere. It had been that way for generations. Edomite had seen many a prince leave through its backdoor. Now it was *his* turn to go.

He felt a hand on his shoulder.

"Sire, why do you brood?"

Ahab was his friend, servant and counsellor. The two of them had known each other from childhood. Ahab's father was the king's advisor. He had brought his son to play with the prince as a little boy, and the two had known each other ever since. There could not have been greater friends than these. They shared everything; from their thoughts and feelings, to the meat on their plates.

"I have been brooding for months, my dear Ahab, so what makes you think I am going to stop now!"

Ahab grinned and gave his friend's shoulder a squeeze. Corliss sighed.

"It is too close. I cannot sleep for thinking about it." He looked back towards the mist.

"What is out there for me that is not in my father's kingdom? Here I have everything that I could possibly wish for. It scares me that I must be banished from it all forever!"

"Oh come now, Corliss, you know that is not true! It is not a banishment, nor is it forever. You may return."

"After a further twenty-one years! And what am I supposed to have done in that time? Built another kingdom?"

Ahab laughed.

"You will not be alone," he said. "You will have your beloved princess, Mariah."

Corliss allowed himself the pleasure of a smile.

"Yes," he said, "I will have Mariah. But out there, I will have to look after her. Had you thought of that? Because I certainly have. What if I cannot do it? Here we have everything we could possibly want provided for us, including the clothes on our backs and the food in our mouths. And then there is this concept of...what do they call it?"

"Money, sire. Pieces of gold and silver that are exchanged for goods. You will learn how to use it."

"It just seems so strange."

"There are many things in The Land Beyond that are different from here. But I understand there are better, more meaningful things as well."

Corliss nodded, but he looked worried nonetheless.

"Anyway, put that from your mind just now. You have your father's challenge coming up in a day or two, and you must focus your mind on that."

They turned from the cliff-edge and headed back into the forest.

"I still have no idea what this challenge is. Might you know?"

Ahab didn't answer immediately.

"I am not permitted to tell you."

Corliss shook his head.

"Who else knows about this?"

"I am not entirely sure but not many. It is a secret."

The challenge they spoke of was another tradition for the prince of the realm. Before a prince's twenty-first birthday, the king would set his son a challenge, usually to prepare him, mentally, for The Land Beyond. Traditionally it was a hard task to accomplish. One king, for example, had told his son that he could eat nothing 'but the crumbs from my table' for twenty-eight days, until the great birthday banquet. This had been to teach him that although he was eating only morsels that usually would not satisfy a grown man, nevertheless those morsels were coming from his father's table; therefore, they would never cease to satisfy.

"Will I enjoy it?" asked Corliss.

"I could not say, sire."

"Stop calling me that!" said Corliss, playfully cuffing him round the ear.

Ahab laughed. "You are the prince of this realm, Corliss. I am your subject and servant!"

"And my best friend. There is no need to say it when we are alone. Besides, I know you are only mocking me!"

Ahab grinned. "The other secret!"

The two of them looked at each other for a long time as they walked, but neither spoke.

The forest floor was a soft blanket of moss and their footfall made no sound. High above and around them was a sea of rich green foliage. The smell of moist undergrowth in the early morning dew lay thick in the air. Exotic plants bloomed with every colour in existence. Bird calls echoed through the tall trees and the sound of a nearby stream could be heard through the stillness.

The Forest of Phoenicia was an area dedicated to contemplation. It was known for its glorious purple flowers that often adorned the head of a bride on her wedding day. Several species of birds dwelled in the forest with the most popular of those being the golden thebany, a nocturnal species which produced a beautiful and soothing sound, which had, on many occasions, caused people to sleep.

"I have often wondered how different my life would be had my father not made that decision," said Ahab. "A risky plan, it has to be said."

"But one, I hope, that has not affected our friendship?" replied Corliss.

"Of course not," said Ahab, frowning. "Why would you think that?"

Corliss shook his head. "I don't know."

They came to the stream that meandered its way through the forest, down from the great mountains. Its water was ice cold and crystal clear and very refreshing to drink.

Corliss stared into it.

"What is the matter, my friend?" asked Ahab.

"It is nothing," he said, "only a dream I have been having recently. And it is not a sweet dream."

"Tell me about it," said Ahab.

"There is a waterfall; large and imposing, throwing out great clouds of vapour. The roar of the tumbling water fills my ears. But it is a strange sound. An element of the roar is human, like somebody screaming."

"A man or a woman?" asked Ahab, quietly.

"A man."

"What is he saying?"

"I cannot make it out. But he is angry. The anger is directed at me."

The stream trickled by.

"Anger is an alien emotion to me. I have heard the king speak of it before as a negative feeling, but it is not one that I have ever experienced."

"Nor I. Nor anybody who has never left the kingdom, Corliss. Only in The Land Beyond do you experience anger, my friend." Ahab paused. He looked troubled now.

"But why do you feel this dream has anything to do with us?"

Corliss looked at him.

Ahab's expression changed. "It is *my* voice that you are hearing in the waterfall! Is it not?"

"It is."

Ahab looked into the trees. He stood silently for a long time. At last he said, "We grew up together, Corliss. We played with the same toys. We played the same games. I feel nothing but love towards you." He turned. "The fact that I should have been prince and not you has made no difference. That was the idea. To swap us round at birth; to let you be a prince and I be your servant. And thus for us to understand that we are both equal, as with everybody else. We are *all* the king's children. Why would I feel resentment?"

"I cannot explain. It is just a feeling." He sighed heavily. "Perhaps it is just my fears solidifying. I do not know what has been happening to me over these past weeks. Every part of me feels different, like I am already detaching myself from Amal and from all that is good. Am I glimpsing the future, Ahab? Is that what this is?"

"It is your mind preparing itself for the unknown."

"I have never seen this waterfall before, and that is the other thing. I usually dream about things I have seen. But I have not seen this waterfall, and it is not a waterfall in Amal; I have seen all of *them*. No, this is different; this is fierce. But if I have not seen it, then where is it coming from? The deepest recesses of my mind, the ones I haven't explored yet?"

Ahab sighed.

"I do not have that answer, Corliss."

Corliss closed his eyes. Then he opened them again quickly, crouched down and splashed the crystal clear water on his face. He instantly felt more revitalised and clearer in his head. He stayed where he was, the water dripping off his hand, back to the source.

"There is another dream as well. This one is not bad; it is pleasant. There is a circular room. The walls are of pale sandstone. In the centre of the room there is an oak table. In the centre of that there is what looks like a chess board, ingrained into the wood. The pieces are set up on either side. There are eight high-backed chairs positioned around this table. One of them is red; the others, white. They are decoratively carved, as if by a highly skilled craftsman. Behind the red chair is a red silk curtain. I cannot see what is beyond it, but I know there is a recess or perhaps another room. There are people waiting in that room to be called forth. The room feels so familiar, as if I have been there many times before. It feels like *my* room, *my* space. The chair is *my* chair. I sit in it every time I come. The room feels official, as though whatever I go there for, is important."

Corliss stared into the water; his eyes glazed.

"And what *is* the reason for you being there?"

Corliss thought for a moment.

"To make a series of important decisions." He looked up. "But about what, I do not know!" He dried his hands and stood up. "I am sorry, my friend," he said, clapping Ahab on the shoulder, "I am not good company at the moment!"

"I am used to that these days."

Corliss chuckled.

"Look around you, sire. Take comfort in all this beauty and peace. Let us just walk, and do what this forest wants us to do, contemplate things. But good things, not bad ones."

Corliss found one of the purple flowers with a little pool of dew cupped in its petals.

Drinking dew from the Phoenicia flower, filled your body and mind with instant invigoration. He picked the flower and tipped the nectar infused water into his mouth.

"I'll take this back for Mariah," he said.

Nearly an hour later they were approaching the main gates of Edomite. These gates were not guarded and were always open. They were quite simply there as an entrance, never to be blocked, always to allow admittance.

They strolled in under the magnificent archway. Corliss now did what he always did when he returned from his morning walk. He headed straight for the little shack that stood just inside the gates, where one could get a breakfast of freshly baked sweet bread, berries and cream.

Jerome, the stall owner, gave him his usual warm welcome, before asking, "Your usual, sire?"

"How did you know?" replied Corliss, grinning.

"What about you, Ahab?"

"I have already eaten."

"You are always up so early, sire. You were out of the gates before I had even opened this morning."

"A restless night, Jerome."

Jerome smiled as he prepared the royal breakfast.

Corliss asked, "How are you? And how is your family?"

"Well, sire; very well."

"I am pleased to hear it."

"But they are always well, sire."

"And I am always pleased."

Jerome laughed.

"Well I am glad to always make you happy." He handed over his breakfast on a wooden plate. "Enjoy it, sire!"

"I will, thank you. Have you been to the main square yet?"

"Indeed I have, sire. I was there a rather long time last night."

Corliss laughed and moved on.

They walked through the streets; Corliss eating and Ahab stealing the occasional berry when his friend was looking in the opposite direction. Everybody they saw greeted them with a respectful gesture; a nod of the head, a bow, a curtsy or a doff of their hats.

Corliss soaked in the familiar sights and smells. Children playing on the cobbles; women leaning out of windows or standing in doorways, talking to their neighbours; animals roaming free, horses, dogs, cats. A rather plump-looking monkey sat on the roof of a fruit stall, stuffing his little face with grapes. A woman was milking a cow, and next to her, a cat sat drinking a saucer of milk that the woman had put aside for it.

"I know I will miss this. The smell of the market; people smiling, dogs barking and the sun shining. It is always so convivial and if you take one more of those berries, Ahab, I will pour cream all over you!"

Ahab laughed.

"I thought we shared everything?"

"I am hungry this morning!"

Ahead of them was the River Mosey that flowed through the city, on the other side of which was the main square. They began to cross the grand bridge, where they paused in the middle to watch the activity along the river bank. It was always teeming with life. A wide grassy slope ran down towards the water's edge. On the south side, this grass gave way to sand and on the north, tall reeds sprung up from the moist earth. Looking towards the north bank, they could see the docks, where craft of all shapes and sizes were moored: schooners, barges and gondolas. Large 'food boats', as they were called, came in from the other cities. The River Mosey passed through each of them and connected them all like one big highway. The food boats brought crops such as barley, corn and wheat from the surrounding fields and olives from the groves that grew on the side of Mount Marwar in the south-west of the kingdom, and finally, apples from the east.

They watched a food boat being unloaded now with great crates of meat being piled up on the docks. The palace's head cook was there, inspecting a large pallet of strawberries. Corliss knew it was a huge delivery for his father's kitchens, some of which was probably to be used in preparations for the great banquet. Elsewhere on the docks, children were diving into the water or messing about in little rowing boats just below it. It was the start of a month long celebration for the prince's twenty-first birthday. Throughout the whole city there was a carnival atmosphere. The fountain in the centre of the main square flowed with wine from morning till night, and a whole series of concerts had been planned, one every evening, in the Royal Concert Hall. People converged on the main square after sunset, dressed as if for a ball, and partied until morning.

Corliss and Ahab entered the main square. Directly ahead of them was the fountain, of white stonework, with angels at the top, pouring what was usually water out of large, ornate jugs. Now it was red wine that tumbled and foamed into the huge pool below.

Two buildings dominated the sky-line here. They were the Royal Concert Hall on one side of the square and the Palace of Edomite on the other. Built entirely of marble, its towers soared high into the air and could be seen for miles around. Each room was a different shade, each bed chamber had its own balcony and the great hall had the largest fireplace in the land.

The palace gardens were open to the public, and many a time had Corliss stood on his balcony and listened to a group of musicians playing directly beneath him, solely for his pleasure.

The people loved their prince. He was good-natured, compassionate and thoughtful.

The Royal Concert Hall, directly opposite the palace, was the height of a ten-story building, circular in shape and boasted a magnificent dome. Known as the 'Diamond Dome', it consisted of a million white diamonds, no bigger than an infant's thumbnail. People came from all over the kingdom to see it. Indeed, many of Amal's citizens were expected to turn up for the celebrations and the seating capacity in the concert hall was three thousand. The audience sat in the round, listening to the musicians on a stage in the centre.

Corliss loved it. He could hardly take his eyes off it now as they strolled slowly through the square. To him, it was the most beautiful building he had ever seen. The marble palace was stunning, but it did not give him the same feeling as he got when he looked at the concert hall. It felt comforting, and it was comforting to be inside it, listening to the heavenly music. He smiled with the knowledge that he would be there this evening for a special concert in his honour, where they would be playing his favourite pieces.

"Let us go to the park?" suggested Ahab.

The park was just off the main square. It was busy as well. Cobbled paths wound their way through immaculate lawns; birch trees with benches wrapped around their trunks; flower-beds bursting with colour; a pond in the middle with a bridge spanning its wide diameter and swans gliding gracefully on the water.

Under a tree nearby was an enormous male lion with its head on a woman's lap, as she combed its great mane.

"Good morning, Adele," said Prince Corliss.

She smiled serenely at the two of them.

"Good morning, Corliss, Ahab."

"Ma'am!" he said, nodding towards her.

"How is your charge?" asked Corliss.

"As happy as ever. He had a slight cough last night, but he is better now."

"He would let you comb that all day, I am sure," said Ahab.

"I intend to. I have nothing else on hand."

The lion yawned now, opening wide its powerful but gentle jaws. It licked the hand that combed it, then settled down again. Adele tickled the big nose and smiled.

"It seems as if he is in no rush either."

Down at the pond a little girl was feeding a swan, while her mother sat cross-legged behind her, plaiting her daughter's hair.

They met Manuel, juggler extraordinaire, at that moment juggling with only ten balls.

"Warming up?" asked Corliss.

Manuel tossed him a ball. Corliss tossed it back to him, and he caught it without breaking his flow.

"Just warming up. I have a show this evening where I will be juggling with fifteen flaming torches, amongst other things."

"Sadly I will miss it, as I have a special concert to attend. But I wish you luck."

"Luck is not a factor!" he replied, throwing the balls even higher.

When Corliss had finished eating, they returned to the palace.

"I must go and see my father," said Corliss, to a footman. "Where is he?"

"He is in the private garden, sire. He waits for you."

"Thank you." He turned to Ahab. "I will see you later my friend."

"Very good, sire," said Ahab, and retreated.

Chapter Four

Hidden Feelings

The private garden was high up amongst the towers, with a fish pool in the centre and a terrace that looked out towards The Land Beyond and the great mountains.

"Good morning, Father."

The king was standing by the wall on the terrace.

"Ah, Corliss, my dear boy, come and have a seat."

Corliss approached his father, who was dressed in his casual morning wear, a loose fitting white shirt and trousers of pink silk. Corliss sat himself down in one of the bamboo chairs and poured himself wine from a carafe on the table. Next to it was a bowl of fruit. His father indicated that he should help himself.

"I have already eaten."

The king sat down next to him.

"It is a fine morning is it not?" he said.

"A fine morning for those who are at peace, Father."

"Are you not at peace?"

"No Father, I am not at peace. And that view does not help."

"Do you not find the mountains beautiful?"

Corliss looked over at him.

"They *are* beautiful, but that is not what I mean. I am afraid, Father. I am afraid to leave here. There is nothing but pain beyond those gates."

"That is not strictly accurate, Corliss. There is also truth and knowledge."

"But you have taught me everything I know, Father!"

"Not everything, my son."

"What else is there to learn?"

"Many things."

His father took an apple from the bowl and bit into it.

"Imagine an orchard in winter, Corliss, a collection of trees with no leaves and no fruit. Close your eyes and envision that for me."

Corliss sighed and closed his eyes.

"The winds blow; the snow falls. The trees are alive, but at the same time, there is no life in them. The orchard is sleeping. But at last, summer arrives. The sun beats down on the orchard, leaves begin to emerge and apples begin to grow. Now each apple consists of a cluster of pips and around that grows the flesh. It is small and sour to begin with, but as time goes by, it grows larger and sweeter. This apple is knowledge, Corliss. The more apples that grow on the tree, the wiser that tree becomes, and it shares that wisdom with the other trees in the orchard."

The king took another bite. Corliss opened his eyes.

"And?" he said, after waiting for his father to continue.

"That is all for the moment," replied the king.

At five o'clock that evening, Corliss reclined in a large marble bath. Plumes of steam rose from the hot water and filled the entire room.

Mariah sat behind his head with her arms around his neck. She was speaking softly to him. "You are a prince, Corliss, you have nothing to fear."

"I do not know how to survive out there, Mariah. And I would far rather you were not coming because I cannot see you go through pain. I will not be able to 'keep' you, and we will struggle to make ends meet. I will speak to my father. You cannot come. Mariah, it is foolish."

"Then I will pine for you every day that you are gone. I will not eat or drink through worry, and I will keep constant vigil until you return."

"No, Mariah, you will be happy, and you will get on with your life here in peace. And one day, when I have completed my tasks, I shall return, and we will be re-united."

He kissed her and she hugged him tighter.

"But I cannot bear to be separated from you, Corliss, my love. I cherish every moment I have with you. You are a part of me, and I know you as well as I know myself. When we marry, we will truly be one. After that I go where you go. I suffer your pain, your anguish. Because that pain is my pain and that anguish, my anguish. You cannot leave me behind."

Ahab stood on the other side of the bathroom door, waiting with refreshments. He listened carefully to the whispered conversation that reached his ears. And as he listened, he began to feel it; the feeling that had been bothering him for months now, uncommon but clearly understood, the feeling of jealousy. He hated it, but he could not stop it from happening. He felt ashamed every time.

He *did* love Corliss like a brother. But that still did not take away from the fact that he, Ahab, was somehow missing out. He understood the plan, but as the years went by, he had begun to disagree with it. It was a decision that had been made without his consent. Everywhere they went now, Corliss received the warm salutations, while Ahab had to stand back and watch, knowing perfectly well that it should be the other way round. Although he knew that in time he would regain his royal status, he still found the role of servant very trying. And that had begun to annoy him intensely.

What annoyed him even more, was that he was passionately in love with Mariah. It should be *him* that she was whispering to now and not his friend Corliss.

He had been in love with her since the day he had set eyes upon her. The king had set up the meeting, which had secretly incensed him. *His* father had given Mariah to Corliss, *his* friend. The imposter. He had been there at their first meeting. The feelings of jealousy and anger had been stronger than they had ever been before.

And yet it was strange. These feelings should not be present in Amal, only in The Land Beyond. But he had never ventured outside the walls; he had never experienced these mortal feelings of anger and jealousy before, so how did he know what they were?

And why did Corliss know about the anger? What was his waterfall dream really about? Did Corliss sense Ahab's true feelings towards him?

Corliss emerged from the bath and stepped into the silk robe, Mariah held out for him.

"Ahab!" he called.

Ahab entered with the refreshments. He laid them on a table by the window which looked down onto the main square.

"Do you need me anymore, sire?"

"Not just now, Ahab. You may go."

With that, Ahab departed.

The king was in his private chambers when Ahab asked audience with him. The servant ushered him in and left them.

"You are angry, my son! Why?"

"You know why!"

The king turned from the window.

"Ahab, what has he got that you haven't?"

"He has Mariah!"

"And why does that matter? You have women."

"I *want* Mariah! She should have been mine! You *gave* her to Corliss! You should have given her to *me.*"

"*Why* should I have? I made the decision to give her to Corliss and now she loves him."

"So you say. You seem to be good at making decisions that mess up my life, Father!"

"You are all my children"

"Enough! I do not want to hear it anymore! If you send me on this challenge with Corliss, upon your head be it if it all goes to hell! Because I have no intention of making it easy for him!"

"I am sorry to hear that. You are his friend, Ahab; you will *need* to help him."

"Then send someone else!"

Ahab turned and stormed out of the room.

The king stood for some time in silence, a strange little smile on his face. Then he looked through the window out onto the central square. A whole host of people were starting to gather now. *His* people. He knew everything there was to know about them; their thoughts, their desires; and even things they didn't know themselves.

He looked across at the Royal Concert Hall with its magnificent dome. It was the heart of the kingdom that building; it brought people together in harmony.

But that was not the only thing it did. The king smiled again. It was not just music that was being conducted within those walls.

He sat in his great chair, lost in peaceful thought. He was thinking about his two boys, Corliss and Ahab. He remembered them as children, playing together in the nursery with its polished marble floors and not a speck of dust in sight. Theirs was a pleasant existence. They had no cares, no worries. Everything that they needed was provided for them. And they had each other.

They would put on plays together, performing them to a large audience in the palace's great hall. They would have singing lessons together, go apple picking during the summer months and snowball fighting during the winter. Jealousy was not an issue back then.

And then one day, when both of them were old enough to understand, the king had sat them down and told them the real situation. They had actually taken it very well.

There had been no bitterness or quarrelling. But perhaps as the years had gone by and the knowledge had begun to sink in, Ahab had begun to feel these negative emotions taking hold. It was part of the plan and exactly what the king had expected.

Ahab, meanwhile, had gone down to the kitchens. He sat on a stool by the range and one of the cooks gave him a mug of hot milk and honey. She had been there a long time and had doted on him as a boy.

He brooded now, as he clasped the hot clay in his hands and caught the soothing aroma of honey from the steam that rose up from the milk. The cook smiled.

"You haven't lost your childish innocence, have you, Ahab?"

"You might think that, Mrs. Garrone. And I wish I could tell you it was true. But it is not. For I am losing the love I once had for my childhood friend, Corliss."

"Nonsense!" replied Mrs. Garrone.

Ahab looked at her.

"Is it? Wouldn't you hate somebody if they had stolen from you?"

"Stolen? What has he stolen from you?"

"My *birthright!"* hissed Ahab, angrily.

Mrs. Garrone frowned.

"What do you mean by that?"

Ahab lowered his voice.

"If I tell you, you must promise not to tell another soul."

"I promise!" she said.

"Corliss is not the true Prince of Amal; I am! My father and *his* father decided that when we were born, we would be swapped round, so that Corliss would experience what it would be like to be prince and I would experience life as his servant. This was designed to make us more tolerant and appreciative of other people when we swapped back to our true roles. They did not tell us about this until we were much older. To begin with, it did not bother me, but now it does. Now I am impatient to have what he has: the title of prince and the girl that comes with that!"

The cook stared at him for a long time in silence. On her face she wore an odd expression.

"You know, Ahab, that is not the first time I have heard this sort of story. There is a similar one. It happened a long time ago and it involved a young prince and his friend, just like you. It is a while since I heard it last and I cannot remember the exact details, but you will find it in the Great Library. It is a tragic story and one that warns about the dangers of jealousy and anger. It is 'The Tale of Araznus and Balthazar'!"

Ten minutes later, Ahab was in a carriage, racing through the streets towards the Great Library. His heart was pounding with a mixture of anger and pure adrenaline.

When he arrived at the library, he dismounted the carriage and marched purposefully into the foyer.

A solitary old man sat in the middle of this large hall, dressed in a long robe. This was the head librarian. Not simply because he was the main man, but because the locations to all the thirty thousand books were in his head.

Ahab walked up to him.

"Head librarian, would you be so good as to point me in the direction of 'The Tale of Araznus and Balthazar'."

Without so much as a pause, the head librarian replied, "Fourth floor, aisle six, shelf seventeen. It is a blue book!"

Mrs. Garrone stirred soup in a big pot over the fire.

"How did he respond?" asked the king.

The cook smiled.

"He shot out of here as though his shoes were on fire, your majesty. You were right; it is working. Well done."

"It is not me that deserves praise; I have nothing to do with this plan. I am only fulfilling my role."

There was nobody around when Ahab reached the fourth floor. He located the book and took it to a table. It was more like a small pamphlet bound in leather. He opened it up and began to read.

This is the tale of two friends, Araznus and Balthazar; one a royal prince, the other, his servant. Both were born

*in the Year of the Crow, only one day apart. Balthazar
was the son of an Edomite silk merchant, who supplied
the king with his wares. The king and the silk merchant
were good friends. Both the queen and the merchant's
wife were expecting children at the same time*

*One evening, while visiting the king, the merchant put
to him a proposition.*

*"Your Majesty," said he, "you are the great leader of
our kingdom, the all-knowing, the all-powerful one. Will
you not therefore do me the honour of bringing up my son
as your own? And in return I will embrace your son as
mine, so I may demonstrate to you how trustworthy I am,
and how far I will go to serve you, Your Majesty."*

*A light came into the king's eyes and he smiled. "That
is a very good proposition. Not only will it demonstrate
your trustworthiness, it will give both boys a different
perspective on life, to the ones they might otherwise have
had."*

*The king agreed to the swap, and once both boys were
born, the changeover was made; under two conditions.
The first was that both of them should become well
acquainted with each other. The second, was that they
should never learn the truth about who they were.*

*So Balthazar grew up in the Royal Palace as a prince,
a very caring boy, eager for knowledge; and Araznus, the
real prince, grew up as the son of a silk merchant. They
were the best of friends. They shared everything, they
played together as children, and each trusted the other for
they had no secrets from each other.*

*When both men were in their twenty-first year, the
king, as is custom, sent his son to The Land Beyond, to
learn more about himself. It was while he was there, and
Araznus still in the kingdom, that his real mother
confessed to Araznus that his life was a lie and that he was*

the real Prince of Amal, and not Balthazar. But she swore him to silence.

Now Araznus was confused and he wanted to speak to his friend without delay. So he gathered together provisions and the meagre amount of gold which he had, and set off with his horse, into The Land Beyond.

As he rode, the confusion about the situation turned to anger and jealousy. Anger over the fact that he had not been told and jealousy of Balthazar's power and status. Perhaps Balthazar had known all along and the trick had been played on Araznus alone. These paranoid thoughts solidified into rage and he urged his horse on, faster and faster.

It took Araznus longer than he expected to find Balthazar. After several years in The Land Beyond, during which he made the most of his changed circumstances, he discovered where Balthazar was living and he sought him out.

It did not take Araznus long to track him down and he unexpectedly found him walking on the road in front of him. He hailed him and Balthazar stepped into the road, assuming that Araznus would slow down. But, Araznus only urged the horse on even faster. Faster he went, and faster, the rage burned like a fire inside his breast; he had never experienced anything like it before.

And then in a flash, it happened: the horse charged Balthazar down, trampling him into the ground. Seconds later, Araznus turned and went back. Balthazar, his childhood friend and confident, was dying before his very eyes.

And suddenly the anger was gone and Araznus realised what he had done. He jumped from the horse and knelt next to Balthazar. He caught the prince's whispered words.

"I thought I was your friend, my dear Araznus?"
And with that Balthazar died.

Araznus was now consumed with guilt. He stayed with his friend's body until it disintegrated into dust. He never ate, slept or drank. His own body became frail and weak. Until finally one morning, as the sun rose over the great mountains, Araznus himself faded away and died.

Their tombstones stand side by side where the two friends perished, a permanent reminder to all those who pass that way, that the emotions of jealousy and anger can have tragic consequences.

Ahab's mouth was dry as he read the words on the page in front of him. Suddenly the room that he was in felt almost eerie. He felt invisible eyes watching him. What was happening now was almost an exact repeat of what happened those many moons ago! What did this mean? He read the story twice more.

Meanwhile, back at the palace, Corliss and Mariah were strolling in the gardens, when a servant came with a message that his father wanted to see him.

When he entered the king's chambers, he found his father standing by the window gazing down into the main square.

"You sent for me?" asked Corliss.

The king turned.

"I know you are nervous about The Land Beyond. It is a big thing for you, as it is for any prince of your age."

Corliss didn't reply.

"Perhaps in order to take your mind off it for just now, you would like to know what your challenge will be?"

Corliss nodded.

"Yes, Father, I would indeed. Though whether it will take my mind off The Land Beyond is another matter."

"That is why my challenge for you involves venturing into that other land."

Corliss' heart began to beat faster.

"What did you say?"

"Instead of having time to worry about it, I will send you out there sooner, so you can become accustomed to it."

Corliss couldn't speak for some time. When he finally did, he asked, "What am I to do when I am out there?"

"I want you to collect something for me. It will mean going on a long journey, a difficult journey, that will lead you to the summit of Mount Tinprelu. There you will find a small wooden hut, next to a lake. In that hut there is a book. A large leather-bound volume with gold leaf. I want you to bring me that book!"

"A book?" asked Corliss.

"Yes."

"You want me to journey to the top of this mountain…for a book?"

"Yes," replied the king, again.

Corliss shook his head in disbelief.

"And what is *in* this book?"

"Ah, that I cannot tell you. You must bring it back with you. And only at the conclusion of the great banquet on your twenty-first birthday, may you learn what is inside."

"And that is my challenge?"

"Indeed. What do you think of it?"

"I think it is the most ridiculous thing I have ever heard!"

"I can understand that. A lot of the challenges kings have set in the past have seemed ridiculous; until they have been completed. I promise you that once you have completed this task, you will understand its purpose."

"Am I to go alone?" asked Corliss.

"No, you will have Ahab with you. So fear not; you will not be abandoned!"

When Corliss and Mariah arrived at the Royal Concert Hall that evening, his mind was most definitely not on the music he would be listening to.

It was a wonderful atmosphere, though, as he walked into the foyer and made his way up the grand staircase to the first floor. Glistening chandeliers hung down from the ceiling.

The building had a fascinating design to it. It was built in concentric circles. In the very middle was the grand auditorium and leading from that, corridors radiated out for fifteen feet through what seemed like a solid mass of thick stone wall that encircled the auditorium. Beyond that, a fine public space with taverns and dining rooms, followed the circumference of the building. The floor was chequered with black and white tiles.

What had always fascinated Corliss were the doors that were positioned at perfect intervals around that thick inside wall. Some of them were washrooms, but the rest of these beautiful mahogany doors were always locked. Were they private chambers for the orchestra? Rehearsal rooms? He did not know.

What he *did* know was that when he tried to open one of these doors he had felt an immense energy that seemed to come from behind it. Immediately he had stepped back. Not because he was afraid, far from it in fact, but out of a sense of respect. That door was not his to open.

As he seated himself next to the king and Mariah in the Royal Box, and gazed around him at the magnificent hall, he began to relax suddenly and enjoy himself. How could he *not* be happy in this awe-inspiring place? He looked down at the circular stage below him. The place was full to capacity. And way above them all, directly above the stage, was the famous diamond dome.

When the orchestra entered, the audience immediately erupted into spontaneous applause. They were followed by the conductor, who, once on stage, turned and made a stately bow towards the Royal Box. The orchestra did exactly the same. The king and Corliss rose together and bowed in return.

The players seated themselves and a hush descended. The conductor took up position and the orchestra raised their instruments in readiness to play.

This was a signal for the lights to fade and complete silence, which continued for what seemed like a couple of minutes.

Corliss sat in the darkness, his whole body now totally relaxed. But his nerves tingled with anticipation. He knew what everybody was waiting for. They were waiting for the clouds to part. And in the next minute they did so. The moon was full. Its silver rays permeated through the million tiny diamonds in the dome and in the next second a brilliant shaft of dancing, dappled moonlight, cut through by the stunning twinkling diamonds, shone down on the orchestra. The conductor made a movement with his baton and music filled the concert hall.

It was one of Corliss' favourite pieces and one that he had heard when he was a boy.

Indeed, it had been a favourite of his friend, Ahab, too. He glanced over at him now, giving him a nod and a smile.

Ahab smiled back, but inside he was scowling. He too remembered this piece, and it reminded him of past times and of innocent times. Of times when they had been true friends.

He reverted his eyes back to the shaft of brilliant light, where he had originally been staring. He was not listening to the music. Instead, he was lost in his own thoughts.

Araznus and Balthazar. Two men just like them. They had played out their lives a hundred years before. And now they were playing it all out again in his mind. From the library he had gone on to the Great Hall of Records, and found out some further things about them. It was Araznus who interested him most, so he removed the diary which Araznus had kept in The Land Beyond. For *his* feelings seemed to mirror Ahab's. Perhaps if he understood the emotions of *this* man, Ahab could understand his own. As he sat in the shadows of the Royal Box, Ahab formed a plan which he would execute in The Land Beyond.

To begin with, Corliss enjoyed the music. But soon his father's challenge began to seep back into his consciousness once more. A *book?* Was his father mad? And so soon! His challenge was to begin in two days' time. He would not sleep tonight; he would be wide awake until morning. He hoped that Mariah would agree to sit up with him and keep him company.

*   *   *   *

Jamie found he was holding his breath. He'd been hanging on Moses' every word. But now the gypsy paused, as he took another gulp of tea.

"What do you think, so far?" he asked. "Enjoying it?"

Jamie nodded. "I like this idea of them swapping round," he said, "but I can see why Ahab is annoyed. Everything has been taken away from him; everything that was his." He thought about that. "Ahab is leading an inferior life to his friend Corliss; but he shouldn't be. Just like I should have had a proper dad, but I don't."

Moses was watching him closely.

"I want Bob to swap places with me; so he can see what it's like from my perspective."

Moses put a hand on the boy's arm. "Are you okay?"

Jamie nodded. Then he seemed to snap out of his gloom. "So these dreams that he's having; are they important?"

"Very much so. These dreams are telling him things that he will come to understand at a later date. Dreams are fascinating. Most of the time they are just jumbled images from our minds. But sometimes they come from elsewhere and contain information that we need to know."

Jamie nodded again.

"Did you understand the symbol of the apple tree?"

"Sort of."

"Explain it to me."

"Well, we are *all* apple trees, and the apples are the lessons we learn."

"In a way, yes. But I'll go into more detail later on."

"So when they enter The Land Beyond, they learn things, right?"

Moses nodded. "Exactly. For example, if you went to another country, you would learn things about the way of life there, which may be different from here in Britain."

"But why don't they learn these things in Amal?"

"It's a bit like school. You're going to learn different

things by going on a field-trip than you would by just sitting in the classroom."

Jamie nodded. "I'm a bit worried about Mariah. She seems to love Corliss, but does she know that Corliss is only the servant? What if she feels cheated by him when she finds out the truth? I know I would." He lowered his head. "That's how I felt when Lauren told me the truth about Bob."

"I understand," said Moses. "It *is* something that Mariah will have to face."

"What is the king's role in all this?" asked Jamie.

"The king is merely there to observe and to make sure that Corliss and Ahab are pushed in the right direction."

"The right direction for what?"

Moses winked at him. "Wait and see," he replied.

Chapter Five

First Impressions

On the morning of the challenge, Corliss rose from his bed, dressed and walked out into the gardens. The gardens were open to the public, and as he strolled in silent thought, a young boy ran up to him and tugged on his coat. Corliss turned.

"Good morning, young sir," he said, with a smile.

"Good morning, Your Highness," replied the boy with a bow. "I brought you something. It is a gift from my father. He made it for you."

The boy handed him a small box, which Corliss opened, to find inside a beautiful gold compass.

"So you will never lose your sense of direction in The Land Beyond."

Corliss smiled again. He was very touched by the gift.

"You may tell your father that it is very much appreciated."

"I am pleased. My family and I wish you luck with your challenge and hope that you are successful."

And with that, the boy bowed again and disappeared. Corliss watched him go. After a moment he resumed his walk. He turned the compass over in his hand, admiring it. It reminded him just how much his people loved and supported him, and it gave him a sense of determination and comfort.

The king had given Ahab a map of the route they were to take. There were several signposts along the way that they were to look out for, signposts that would confirm they were on the right path. Food and provisions had been organised and transportation in the form of two horses was provided.

With Mariah at his side, Corliss now looked towards Edomite's back gates. In less than three hours those gates would be opening, and he would get his first impressions of The Land Beyond.

When that moment finally came, it looked like the whole city had turned out to bid him farewell.

Ahab was busy securing the provisions onto the horses.

"Are you ready for this?" he asked.

"As ready as I will ever be," replied Corliss.

A gong was suddenly sounded and silence fell.

"Citizens of Edomite!" shouted the king. "I thank you all for turning up this morning, to wish my son luck on his great challenge. Once again we witness the continuation of an ancient tradition. These traditions are important to us all for they make us who we are." He turned to Corliss. "I too, wish you luck, my son. And I shall see you next on your birthday!"

As the gates slowly opened, it felt like the whole city was holding its breath. The sun was just coming up over the Great Mountains and Corliss caught his first glimpse of the alien landscape he was to journey through.

Mariah gripped his hand one last time, kissed both him and Ahab on the cheek, and slipped back to join the throng of well-wishers.

Corliss stepped forward slowly beyond the gates, Ahab by his side, pulling the horses. As the gates closed behind them, Corliss stood very still, listening. There was complete silence. A cool breeze blew on his face in the early morning light.

At first it didn't seem too different to that of Amal. There were a few plants and trees he hadn't seen before, and the path that wound its way through the shrubbery ahead of them was more rugged and stony.

"Well?" said Ahab, finally.

Corliss looked at him.

"I am out. I have done it." Again, he looked around him. "It feels very strange."

"Let us walk," said Ahab. "Let us get used to the place."

They began to walk slowly along the path, Corliss looking at absolutely everything.

He picked flowers and sniffed them; he picked up rocks and examined them. Ahab watched him without a word, just letting him experience what he wanted to.

Up ahead, Corliss suddenly caught sight of a deer, grazing on the foliage. In a child-like movement, Corliss ran up to it; for Corliss loved all animals, and all animals loved him. But not this one, and as soon as it saw him, it bolted. Corliss stopped dead.

"Why did it do that?"

"Animals here are afraid of humans."

"Why?"

Ahab shrugged.

"It is The Land Beyond."

Corliss sighed.

"Do you have the map?"

Ahab produced it.

"Which direction are we going in?"

"For the moment, straight on. Our first port of call is the Lake of Karma. It lies at the bottom of the foothills that lead up into the Great Mountains. It is there we shall meet the Lady of the Lake."

"Who is she?" asked Corliss.

"She is a water spirit, one of the oldest there is. She blesses all those who travel into the mountains."

The sun rose higher into the sky as the two men walked side by side along the path.

"So which is Mount Tinprelu?" asked Corliss, looking at the Great Mountains on the horizon.

"The tallest one!" replied Ahab, pointing.

Corliss stared at the ominous mountain that rose several hundred feet higher than its neighbours. He swallowed. His father was right; it was going to be a long and difficult journey.

By midday they had walked ten miles, through landscape that hardly changed. But Corliss hadn't been thinking about the landscape for some time now. Instead he had been pre-occupied with the pain in his feet and ankles.

"Can we rest, Ahab; there is something wrong with my feet."

They stopped and Corliss sat down on a tree stump.

"It is normal," said Ahab. "When you walk this far here, your joints and muscles get tired. That is why we have the horses."

"Won't *they* get tired?"

"They are far stronger than we are."

"How do you know all this?" asked Corliss.

"Your father has been describing the conditions to me for some weeks now."

Corliss nodded.

"How long until we reach the lake?" he asked.

Ahab looked at the map; then looked around him and back at the map.

"Er…well, we are probably about here, so, maybe another sixty miles? It looks like we've done ten so far."

"I think we will use the horses from now on," said Corliss.

They unpacked some food and ate it in the sunshine.

"Apart from the discomfort in my ankles," said Corliss, "it is really not that bad here after all."

He watched a bird flying overhead; listened to the song it sang. It was remarkably peaceful, he thought.

When they had finished eating and Corliss had rested, they mounted the horses and continued on their journey.

After a further twenty-five miles, the horses were tired, not to mention their riders. It was also beginning to get dark.

"We will stop here for the night," said Ahab.

Chapter Six

A Restless Night

They set up camp just off the road, on a small patch of grass that was free from shrubbery. Ahab found wood for a fire and the horses were tied to a nearby tree. The sun sank behind the mountains, and a brilliant starry sky appeared. They sat next to the fire and ate their evening meal, before settling back for the night in their fur-covered sleeping sacks.

But it was difficult to sleep when there was so much to think and talk about.

Corliss gazed up at the sky above him, his hands behind his head.

"Do you realise," he said, "this is the first time we have been on a true adventure together."

Ahab nodded. "You are right. There have been many excursions to exotic places in Amal, but they never felt like adventures."

"Because we knew it belonged to the king and we were ultimately safe. Here it is different; this place has rules of its own. It does not abide by the rules of Amal. The king has no control here. And that is what an adventure truly is: going somewhere and doing something that is a risk." He nodded to himself. "I am glad he has sent us on this adventure, however fruitless it may seem."

Corliss frowned.

"What is it?" asked Ahab.

"My father was talking about knowledge the other day. He described it as being like an apple on a tree. The more apples the tree had, he said, the wiser that tree would be. I thought I *was* wise. Perhaps not. Perhaps by having adventures I can grow more apples and gain in wisdom."

"Exactly!" replied Ahab. "Why do you think each king has sent his prince into the unknown? To hope that he learns."

"But what is he supposed to learn? And does the king already know it? If so, why does he not simply tell him the answers?"

"That is a good question, and one to which I do not have the answer. Yet!"

"Corliss smiled and mused, "You always thought you had the answers to things. Even as a boy. You were always reading; always asking questions and searching for the answers. You have always been more intelligent than me."

Ahab thought for a moment on that statement. It seemed to trigger something. Up until now he had thought that Araznus, a commoner like himself, was the man who mirrored his own emotions. But Balthazar had been fascinated by the pursuit of knowledge, which Araznus had not. Interesting!

"That it not strictly true, Corliss. You know some things that I don't."

"Such as?" asked Corliss.

"Such as what it is like to be the leader of a great realm."

"I am not the leader, the king is. I suppose I have an element of responsibility towards Amal's citizens, but…"

"What is it like to be admired by so many people?" asked Ahab.

Corliss was silent a moment.

"You can feel it. Feel their love. It is like thousands of tiny fish all gently nibbling at you. But it is not painful. Each time they nibble it is like warm knitting needles kneading at your skin."

Ahab did not respond immediately.

"How pleasant for you. Except I did not ask what their love feels like. I asked about their admiration."

"But with admiration comes the love," replied Corliss.

"Is that so?" replied Ahab.

His face was half shrouded in shadow, so Corliss did not see his angry expression. He changed the subject now.

"We should reach the lake in two days. From there the journey will be up hill and more difficult. So we must get plenty of rest. Goodnight, Corliss."

"Goodnight, Ahab."

Ahab rolled over onto his side and said no more. Corliss gazed at the fire. It was a comfort out here in the wilderness. He could hear the horses in the darkness, chomping away on their grass. At least *they* were calm and content. For an hour, Corliss lay on his back and tried to sleep, but it didn't work. Something was bothering him. It was the dream about the waterfall when he had felt Ahab's anger. What did it mean? Was it merely his fears solidifying as Ahab had suggested? Or was Ahab upset with him for some reason? But if so, why would that be? They had been friends all their lives, good friends. There had never been any disagreements between them. Corliss sat up. The air was quite cold, but not too bitter, he thought. Bitter? What if Ahab was bitter about the situation after all? What if he wanted to be prince? Surely he would have said if that was the case; they never had secrets between them. Or perhaps he was just being paranoid. It was all the worry that was making him think like this.

He stood up and went over to speak to the horses. Talking to animals always made him feel comforted. Horses were especially receptive to his voice. Perhaps *they* found it soothing, too? He stood between them now, stroking their means and talking softly to them. They almost immediately began to nuzzle him.

Suddenly, Corliss heard a crack, a little way off in the trees. He started. He stepped round the back of the horses and peered into the darkness. He could not see or hear anything, but his heart was pounding.

"Calm down!" he told himself. "It is an animal, most likely."

He was aware that the inhabitants of The Land Beyond were not always friendly.

He had never experienced hostility from a fellow Amalian. How would he cope with hostile people here? He had Ahab with him, yes, but what if there were more of them?

He went back to tending the horses. A few minutes later though, there was another crack, and this time it sounded closer. Again, Corliss peered round the tail end of the horses.

And now he could see something, the unmistakable silhouette of a man. He was standing at the edge of the trees, perfectly still. Although Corliss could not see his face, he knew the man was watching him. Corliss, too, stayed perfectly still. His body began to shake. He had felt this before but not here. He had felt it a long time ago, as a small boy. For several moments the two of them stared at each other. Neither spoke nor made a movement. And then all at once the figure took a step forward. Corliss' heart leapt up into his throat, followed by something on his throat; a cold, sharp metal blade.

At the same time a hand was placed over his mouth; a hand that was almost as cold as the blade itself. And then a coarse voice whispered in his ear.

"Let's not wake the other one!"

Corliss couldn't move. His limbs were frozen. The other man approached.

"What have they got?"

"Food! Good food! And drink; I've had a look in the saddle bag. We'll eat like kings tonight!"

His accomplice smiled.

"We'll take the horses as well."

"How many will that take us up to?"

"Ten; one for each of us!"

"The lads will be pleased!"

"Aye, that they will!"

"What else have you got, boy?" asked the man who held him. "Any money?"

Money? Was that? Of course. Corliss shook his head. Ahab had the money on his person. It was agreed that he would keep hold of it.

"I don't believe you. Your clothes are wealthy. Search the…"

His speech was abruptly cut off. At the same time his accomplice suddenly turned tail and fled back into the trees. The other man's hand slipped from Corliss' mouth and he slumped to the ground. Corliss turned.

Ahab stood there, holding a bloodied knife.

"That is something else you can do here. Kill a man!"

Corliss stared at his friend, then looked down at the body.

"This one won't be troubling us again. But the rest of them will. We must keep a vigil during the nights. And I must teach you to use this." He held up the knife. "I will keep watch tonight," he said.

Chapter Seven

Where All Roads Lead

Corliss eventually managed to get some sleep, if only a few hours. When he woke, Ahab was cooking breakfast over the fire. Corliss smiled as he caught the waft of sausages.

"I am glad they did not get those!"

Ahab nodded, but his face was sour.

"They got some other stuff, though."

Corliss sat up. "What do you mean?"

"I must have dozed off. I am truly sorry."

"What did they get?"

"Three bottles of wine, two bags of oats, most of the goats' cheese and three loaves of bread. I woke too late, and they were way off into the trees."

"So how much do we have left?"

"Not enough to get us to the next village on our route. We would have to veer off on another path that comes up at a crossroads, about five miles ahead. But that will put us back by…"

He paused.

"By how long?" asked Corliss.

"A day, two days!"

"It is what we will have to do. We have no choice in the matter."

"If you say so," replied Ahab.

When breakfast was finished they were back on the road. They went slowly with the horses nodding along beside each other as though they were having a conversation.

Something Corliss and Ahab were definitely not doing. All through breakfast, Corliss had been thinking about the theft. It seemed so strange; the choice of food they had taken.

Strange, because goats' cheese and wine were two things that Ahab was very fond of.

It was only Ahab's word that they had come back. And then he had pulled himself up short. Why would he doubt Ahab's word anyway? It was not right to do such a thing.

He must not do it again, he told himself.

Ahab seemed to have sensed his thoughts, for he said, "Are you angry with me?"

"What?"

"Angry…at me, for dozing off?"

"Of course not, my friend. When have I ever been angry with you?"

"Never. But remember it is different now that we are here. Our emotions will change. Do not forget that."

Corliss nodded but said nothing. They continued on for a bit in silence.

"Why should that be?" asked Corliss, suddenly.

"Why should what be?" asked Ahab.

"Why should we get angry with each other?"

"We get angry when one person has wronged another," replied Ahab, his eyes not straying from the road.

"What do you mean by 'wronged'?"

"Let's use, for example, the two men last night. They were trying to steal from us. Stealing is taking things that do not belong to us, when we do not have consent to take them."

Corliss frowned. "But everything belongs to everybody, surely?"

"Does it? When I took those berries from you the other day, did those not belong to you, as that was your breakfast?"

"Ahab, I normally share it with you. I was just hungry. I told you that. If I had passed that plate to you, with the berries still on it, it would have been *your* plate and therefore *your* breakfast and *your* berries."

"But why do we say that everything in Amal belongs to everybody equally?"

"Because everything in Amal belongs to the king. And he has stated, like every king before him, that everything that belongs to him, belongs to every citizen of Amal."

"Precisely," replied Ahab, "and therefore there is no need to steal. But in The Land Beyond, there is no such ruler, and therefore no such rule. So what belongs to one man here, does not necessarily belong to his neighbour. Do you understand?"

Corliss nodded.

"And so, if a man wants his neighbour's cow, and that neighbour refuses to give it to him, the man might *steal* his cow. And that is wrong!"

"And so the neighbour whose cow was stolen becomes angry with the man who has stolen?"

"That's correct."

"I see. And you have learned this through your studies?"

Ahab nodded.

"What else have you learned?"

Ahab shook his head.

"Later," he said. "We still have a long journey ahead of us."

They reached the crossroads two hours later and halted the horses. Just next to the crossroads was a little stone cottage with a thatched roof. Next to that was a wooden sign-post with four arrows. Ahab studied them. He pointed off to his right.

"That way; but it's longer than I thought." Ahab sighed. He looked at his friend. "It's your choice."

"We need provisions. My decision is unchanged."

Ahab nodded.

"I wonder where the other roads lead?" said Corliss out of curiosity.

"All roads ultimately lead to the same place," said a voice.

Ahab and Corliss turned their heads at the same time. Just coming round the side of the cottage was a little old lady in a tattered dress and shawl. In her left hand she held a bucket and with her right, she was scattering oatmeal on the ground, where a cluster of hens were gobbling it ravenously.

"Good morning, ma'am," said Corliss.

"Good morning, gentlemen."

"What were you saying?" asked Corliss.

"I was saying that at the end of the day, all roads lead to the same place."

"What do you mean?"

The old lady chuckled.

"Oh never mind, just an old woman's strange ramblings. Which way were you going?"

"Towards the town of Sparttul, ma'am," replied Ahab.

"Oh well, you'll enjoy that place. There is great entertainment there for young men like you."

"Actually we are only there to pick up supplies," interrupted Corliss.

"What sort of entertainment?" asked Ahab, sounding interested.

"There are some very good taverns, dance halls, smart accommodation, and it's all there for the taking in Sparttul."

Ahab grinned.

Corliss was staring at the old woman. "Your clothes, ma'am, they are worn. Why is this?"

"I do not have the money to buy new material," she replied, matter-of-factly.

Corliss frowned.

"Oh," he said, not quite understanding.

"I am not wealthy like you gentlemen."

"Well we must give you some of *our* money," said Corliss.

Ahab looked at him askance.

"Ahab, give her some of the gold coins for clothes and some for food. You need not be poor, ma'am."

"But, Corliss…"

"Now, Ahab."

Ahab grudgingly reached into a pouch on his belt and handed her five gold coins. The old lady received them gratefully and eagerly with ravaged hands.

"My blessings to you, good sir," she said to Corliss.

"Good day to you, ma'am."

As they rode off in the direction of Sparttul, Ahab was shaking his head.

"What is wrong, Ahab?"

"We *need* that money, Corliss. You cannot just get rid of it so frivolously. Some people are poor, and some are rich. That is not our problem. Here we must look out for ourselves."

"We have plenty of money, Ahab. Why should she not have some of it?"

"Plenty!" repeated Ahab. "How much do you think we have?"

Corliss shook his head.

"I don't know."

"That's right; because you have no idea how money works. That's why I am in control of it. And why I know that because this is all we have, each penny counts."

It took them an entire day of riding until they reached the town of Sparttul at seven o'clock in the evening.

As they rode in through the main gates, the town seemed alive with fun and laughter.

Taverns overflowed with drinkers, a throng of people on the streets and coaching inns advertised cheap rooms. Ahab beamed.

"Just the kind of welcome we need at the end of a long day!" He looked at Corliss, who was not smiling. "Relax, Corliss, what's wrong with you?"

"Nothing; I am just tired, that is all. I hope there is still a room somewhere. I would prefer to sleep in a nice warm bed tonight, rather than out in the open. Our first priority must be to find accommodation."

They rode slowly through the crowds, looking for something suitable. At last, they found somewhere above a tavern. The landlord, seeing that they were wealthy travellers, personally escorted them up to their rooms. Ahab's was directly across the corridor from Corliss'. Their horses had been put in the stables round the back.

"What time do the markets open tomorrow?" asked Corliss.

"Nine o'clock, sir."

"Thank you."

"Will you be requiring dinner this evening, gentlemen?"

"Yes, please," replied Corliss. "As soon as possible!"

Chapter Eight

A Dark Deal

They were shown to a table in the crowded tavern downstairs. No sooner had their food arrived, than Corliss tucked straight in. He was famished. It felt so good to be warm, to be in shelter and to have a hearty plate of hot food in front of you. As he ate, he felt that he had never enjoyed a meal so much. It was the combination of being finally rested from a tiring journey, his limbs stiff, his eyelids heavy. He felt grateful.

In Amal he had eaten many great feasts, but he had never fully appreciated how wonderful a simple hot meal could be.

He ignored everything around him for ten minutes, as he polished off his plate. At last he sat back, took up his wine glass and observed the melee of people.

"I am sorry for my glumness," he said, to Ahab. "I am glad we came here."

Ahab grinned at him. "We have plenty of time. And if I hadn't fallen asleep, we wouldn't need to be here. Funny how things happen, isn't it?"

Corliss laughed. He ordered another plate of food and twenty minutes later, another carafe of wine. But eventually his eyelids became even heavier and he had to retire to bed.

"I'm going to stay here for a while," said Ahab.

"We should get started early tomorrow," said Corliss.

As Corliss moved away through the swarm of bodies, Ahab scowled in his direction. "He still thinks he can tell me what to do, even here!" said Ahab to himself. He poured the rest of the carafe into his glass. Last night he had deliberately eaten the bread and cheese and leisurely drunk the three bottles of wine. Why? Why shouldn't he? Why should he not enjoy himself? After all, as far as Corliss was concerned, the food was as much Ahab's as it was his. It also gave him an excuse to come to Sparttul. Here he could have what he wanted. Here, he could be a prince.

Ahab had no intention of doing what the king had instructed him to do. He had thrown away the oats to make it look like a theft. But he had a funny feeling Corliss knew what he had done. When he had finished the wine, he left the tavern to explore the rest of the nightlife.

Meanwhile, Corliss lay in his bed, under his warm blankets, and stared out of the window at the large moon that hovered over the town. Was his father staring at the same moon, he wondered?

Corliss' heart was heavy. There was something different about his friend now; something he had not experienced before. It felt as if Ahab and he were very slowly drifting apart. He did not feel that Ahab's feelings towards him were as warm as they had once been. Ahab was talking to him differently; his tone was harsher. Was it he who had eaten the bread and cheese last night? Why was he, Corliss, having doubts about his friend's honesty?

He thought suddenly of Mariah. Did she truly love him? Mariah had no idea about the plan. As far as Mariah was concerned, she was in love with the prince. Did it matter to her that the prince was really the servant?

He thought back to the time when he and Ahab had been boys; when they had been inseparable. He had assumed that would always be the case.

Corliss suddenly felt compelled to go and talk to Ahab about this. He rose quickly and went back down to the tavern. But he had gone. He went out looking for him. He delved into tavern after tavern, pushing through revellers, tripping over drunkards, until he finally found him.

Ahab was sitting at a table. But he wasn't alone. A pretty, young girl was sitting on his lap and Ahab was running his fingers through her mass of red curls. Up on a stage, a group of girls were dancing as a band played a jig. Corliss approached him.

"Ahab, we need to talk!"

"Corliss! Meet Jessie. Jessie is a dancer, among other things."

"Now, Ahab!"

"You must forgive my friend, Jessie, he's a little uptight at the moment; he needs to…'

"I *need* to *talk.*"

"Then talk!"

"In private; preferably somewhere quieter!"

"Can't it wait; I'm a little busy just now?"

"No, it can't."

Ahab kissed Jessie on her ruby red lips.

"Will you excuse us for a minute, my sweet?"

"Just for a minute!" she replied.

When she had gone, Ahab said, "Don't think that you can tell me what to do anymore, Corliss! I'm not your servant now!" He stood up. "Amal is seventy miles east. Here, I do what I please!"

"Then why don't you take the rest of the bread and cheese!" snapped Corliss.

"Maybe I will." He chuckled. "You know I never realised quite how pathetic you were, until now! You can't do anything without me! Why don't you go back to bed… *prince*? I have some business to attend to!"

Corliss stared at him. He watched him walk away with the girl, his arm round her shoulder.

Corliss sat down slowly. He felt weak. Suddenly water began to drip from his eyes.

He wiped it away, but more came. There was an odd feeling in his heart now. He didn't realise it was sadness.

Ahab and the girl entered a room where she locked the door behind them. "No one will disturb us here," she said.

"That's very true!" said a gruff voice.

Ahab stopped breathing as three rough looking men stepped out of the shadows. The man who had spoken held a large dagger. Ahab swallowed.

"What do you want?" he managed to ask. "Money? I have plenty of that."

"Sounds good. But we want something else as well."

"What's that?"

"Blood for our blood, my friend!"

Ahab's heart started to beat ten times faster.

"Now just wait a minute," he said, starting to shake.

"'Fraid I haven't got a minute; and neither have you!"

The man leaped forward. Ahab dodged out of the way and made a dash for the door.

He grabbed the key and tried to turn it, but he was gripped from behind and thrown to the floor.

"Let me make a deal!" he cried.

"What deal do you think you can make with us that will spare your life?"

"I'll give you three hundred gold coins, and I'll give you blood; but not mine!"

"Whose?"

Ahab paused only for a second.

"My travelling companion's!"

The man hesitated.

"And where is he?"

"He was in the tavern, last I saw. But you mustn't do it here. I have an idea if you'll let me explain."

Ahab delved into his pouch and removed a folded -up piece of parchment. Slowly he got to his feet, went over to a small table with a candle on it and laid the parchment out flat. It was a map.

"This is our route, gentlemen. We're headed for the summit of Mount Tinprelu. Or at least, *he* is!"

"What do you mean by that?"

"I have a separate agenda. Corliss thinks he's following a different map; one his father gave me. That's long gone. I was supposed to go with him; instead I will accompany him as far as this point here..." Ahab pointed to a spot on the map, "and then I will abandon him. He will have to go the rest of the way on his own." Ahab straightened up. "And that is when you will ambush and kill him. Then I will meet you here, at the village of Greystone, and you will get your money!"

The man scratched his head, thoughtfully.

"And just what makes you think I can trust you?"

"Because I am Prince Ahab. My servant and I have come from the city of Edomite, capital of the great kingdom Amal, ruled by my father. That is why you can trust me. My servant is a traitor and he deserves to die."

The man nodded slowly.

"Well my name is Hanson. It's an honour to meet you, Prince Ahab from Edomite."

He shook Ahab's hand. Then grasped it firmly. "But even so, I'll be wanting something more concrete than just your *title*. So, here's what I propose. I take the three hundred gold coins off your hands now, kill your traitor and then you give me another three hundred after that. How does that sound? After all, a prince shouldn't have any trouble coughing up six hundred gold coins should he?"

"Of course not," replied Ahab, a little stiffly.

"Now let's just suppose, merely for argument's sake you understand, that when it came to handing over that extra three hundred, you suddenly felt obliged to decline. We would have to have a back-up plan, if you like, which would make sure that didn't happen."

Ahab swallowed. "I suppose you would."

Hanson smiled. He walked over to Jessie, who was being held by one of his men. Her face was ashen grey. Hanson raised his dagger hand to her hair and cut off a few of those perfect curls.

"Why don't you keep this as a reminder of how beautiful this young woman is? And as a reminder that if you don't want me to detach anything else from her person, you'll give me that extra three hundred. Now, are we understanding each other, Mr. Prince?"

"Perfectly!" replied Ahab, as he slipped Jessie's hair into his pocket. He then handed over the pouch of money, which Hanson counted, and headed for the door.

"Until Greystone, gentlemen," he said, and left the room.

Hanson chuckled. "Now that's what I call a deal!"

"You should have just killed him when you had the chance!"

"And lose out on six hundred gold ones; don't be daft! If you want to be leader of this gang one of these days, Jeremiah, you're going to have to learn how to get more out of a situation than you otherwise would."

"Thank you for my impromptu haircut, by the way," said Jessie, sullenly.

Hanson smiled, "The punters ain't going to notice anything, my angel, and you've got plenty left. Besides, now I have a guarantee, and it means I can snuff out two instead of one and be six hundred pounds richer. I think this calls for a celebration!"

*   *   *   *

"I know what you're trying to do," said Jamie.

Moses stopped talking. "What is that?"

"You're trying to show me how this story relates to my life. Corliss and Ahab are falling out, just like me and the rest of my family. Ahab is scheming against his old friend; things are changing. They're changing for me too. I used to think I had two parents; now I'll never be the same again."

"You're right, Jamie, this story does relate to you. That's why I'm telling it. You are angry with your sister for telling the truth. You are angry at Bob for his treatment of you. Some truths, when learned, can do that. But anger is part of the learning process and has to be experienced, no matter how painful it is."

"But at the moment, Corliss doesn't seem to be learning much. I thought you said he was going to learn things in The Land Beyond?"

Moses held up his hand. "Patience, Jamie. You need to listen to the whole story."

Chapter Nine

The House of Araznus

Ahab returned to his bedchamber above the tavern and quietly closed the door. He sat down slowly on the bed. The pouch had contained three hundred and forty gold coins. Hanson had let him keep the forty, so there was plenty left for shopping tomorrow. But that was all they had. How on earth was he going to get his hands on another three hundred?

He lay down now and stared up at the ceiling. The only possible way was to steal it. He suddenly rolled over and delved into the animal-skin bag he carried with him, and removed a little book. It was the diary of Araznus which he had 'borrowed' from the Hall of Records. He now opened it to the first page and began to flick through it, looking for the most relevant passages.

I am preparing to leave Amal; I must find my friend. I must understand this situation. I cannot believe that all along he has been taking my place as Prince of the Realm. Why would our parents do that to us?

Ahab flicked on a little more.

Did he know that I was the real prince? Did everybody know? Is this joke on me? And why?
I am in Sparttul, a town of lavish behaviour. I am a jilted prince. Here I will seek what I did not have in Amal.

Respect! I will seek entertainment worthy of Royalty. Let Balthazar flounder on his own for once. I trust his life is not as rosy as it once was. I can wait. As long as I have comfort and good food here. Perhaps I will purchase a house? A big house! I will fill it with servants who will wait on me hand and foot. I will be ruler there; king and prince all in one! People will bow to me! I will throw wild parties so that people will know my name and know me to be a great person. I will take back what I had stolen from me; I will reclaim my birthright!

Ahab had already read this; but to read it again was just as powerful. This man's thoughts were his own. He was not alone; the ghost of Araznus hovered over his shoulder. He wanted to follow Araznus on his journey; retrace his steps; visit the same places and understand why he felt the way he did in those places. "Lead me on my own journey of discovery, Araznus. Show me the stars that light my way when everything else is dark."

Early the next morning, he stood outside a huge mansion in the centre of town.

"The House of Araznus!" he said, to himself. "You were here, my friend, and you would have stood where I am standing now." He cast his eyes over the grand facade. "Let me enter your abode!"

A brass name-plate informed him that it now belonged to Sir John Mayfield. He went forward and knocked on the great oak door. It was presently opened by a servant.

"May I help you, sir?"

"Forgive me for calling so early, but I wish to see Sir John."

"Do come in."

Ahab stepped into the great front hall.

"May I ask who is calling?"

"Prince Ahab of Amal!" replied Ahab, in a stately voice.

"If you will kindly wait here, I will inform Sir John of your presence." When the servant had departed, Ahab stared around him at the grandeur. This must have been where Araznus held his wild parties.

"Prince Ahab?" said a voice.

He turned. A gentleman was descending the main stairs.

"Good morning, Sir John."

"I do not believe I have had the pleasure before. How can I be of service, Your Highness?"

"My dear Sir John, you may not have heard of me, but I have most definitely heard of you. And the original owner of this grand property."

"The great Araznus!" said Mayfield, beaming. "He was quite a character."

"I am his descendant."

Mayfield stared at him and bowed. "Then your presence in my house is even more of a pleasure."

"I will come straight to the point. I am travelling through this land on a very important mission. I left home with limited funds which have since unfortunately run out. I wonder if I may be so bold as to…"

"How much do you require, Your Highness?"

"Four hundred gold coins; which will be repaid to you at the earliest opportunity."

"That is not a problem. It will be my pleasure to assist you, Your Highness. Would you like to follow me?"

He followed Mayfield down into the bowels of the house, to the vault; his personal treasure chest. He drew back six different locks and then heaved the door open. Ahab saw mound upon mound of gold coins, piled at least two feet high. He stared in wonderment at the horde. He had never seen anything like it. He had heard stories of enormous wealth in The Land Beyond but had never experienced it for himself until now.

"You could buy anything you wanted with this."

"Yes, indeed," replied Mayfield.

He strolled forward into the vault. On a table was a bundle of bags. He took one now and began counting four hundred gold coins into it.

Just think, said Ahab to himself; I could have all this and more, in a place where wealth matters; where it makes you respected and admired; where it makes you a somebody. Araznus, you must have hated Balthazar so much. You had this house, you had your wealth and your respect; exactly what you wanted. And yet you still wanted revenge. I understand. The hatred I have for Corliss will drive me on until I have everything and he has nothing! Mayfield handed him the bag. "My thanks to you, Sir John."

"Don't mention it, Your Highness. If you wouldn't mind signing this receipt as my accountant is a stickler for protocol."

"But of course! And now may I have a quick look round the rest of my ancestor's house?" asked Ahab. "It would be fascinating to me."

"And it would be my pleasure."

As Sir John led him from room to lavish room, each decorated in its own unique way, Ahab felt something rise in his chest, and it was a strong emotion.

"Now this room I especially love. I think you'll agree that the ceiling in here is spectacular!"

As Ahab looked up, something happened. A shiver passed through his entire body. He froze and was rooted to the spot. He was staring at a thousand gold stars against a dark blue background.

"It's just like looking at the night sky!" remarked Mayfield.

"Yes," agreed Ahab. He spoke slowly, as if in a daze. "There is a part of all of us in the stars. That's why they shine so bright!"

Mayfield chuckled pleasantly.

"Very nicely put, Your Highness."

Ahab looked at him now, as if suddenly remembering he was there.

"Why do I think I've seen this before?" he asked, again tilting his neck to look up. He frowned. "And where on earth did that phrase come from?"

Chapter Ten

The Witches of Marshwind

After his visit, Ahab quickly returned to the inn and managed to prepare the horses before Corliss emerged.

"Good morning, sire," said Ahab, humbly.

"Good morning," replied Corliss.

"Sire," said Ahab, his head lowered. "I apologise for my behaviour last night. Feelings in this place have gone to my head. I will try and behave sensibly from now on."

Corliss embraced him, "I was afraid we were being teased apart. You are my childhood friend, Ahab, and I love you like a brother. Of course I forgive you." Tears of happiness and relief came into his eyes. "You know so much about this place, Ahab. Why do my eyes water?"

"It happens when you get emotional," said Ahab, smiling.

Corliss wiped them away with the back of his hand. "It's a strange place, this."

That was at ten o'clock in the morning. At four o'clock that afternoon, they stood looking down towards the Lake of Karma with its two massive waterfalls plunging into it from a high clifftop, and beyond that, the start of the Great Mountains. The lake itself was a gorgeous, icy turquoise blue.

Corliss and Ahab made their way down the hill towards it. The horses took their time on the dirt path that shifted under their hooves.

As soon as they reached the lake's shore, Corliss was off his horse and down on his knees by the water's edge. He splashed water on his face and neck, for it was a hot day and a long one at that.

Suddenly, about twenty yards out, the surface of the lake began to move and swirl. As Corliss watched, a whirlpool of water rose up into the air. As the water swirled round and round, it seemed to be carving a shape out of itself. Corliss realised he was not looking at a whirlpool, but the top half of a shimmering female form.

"The Lady of the Lake"!" said Ahab.

Corliss stood up now and took a few paces back, as the water spirit moved towards them.

The bottom half of the form was still a column of spiralling water that remained in contact with the lake at all times.

"Greetings!" said the spirit. It spoke with a soft, soothing tone, as soft and gentle as water that trickles down a smooth rock face. "Do you travel into the mountains?" it asked.

"We do!" replied Ahab.

The spirit raised its right hand.

"I bless and protect you with the element of these karmic waters that you may travel safely on your journey through the mountains."

As she spoke, she sprayed them with water.

"Thank you, spirit," said Corliss.

And then the water spirit broke apart in a huge shower of shimmering droplets that hit the surface of the lake like rain. And everything was still again.

"Could we just set up camp here?" asked Corliss. "It's a lovely spot, and we have been travelling a long time."

"It's your decision, sire," said Ahab.

So they set up camp next to the Lake of Karma, in the shadow of the foothills, and early next morning, they began their ascent towards Mount Tinprelu.

They climbed up another rugged pathway next to the waterfall until they reached a plateau with a river running through it.

"Now all we do is follow the river for a couple of days at least. We won't need to worry about losing our bearings for the moment."

"What does the map say?" asked Corliss.

"It says we follow the river for about eighty miles through flat ground, before it starts to ascend higher towards the mountains. At one point we pass through marshland, where we'll encounter a group of settlers in their sinking houses…"

"What?"

"They settled there half a century ago and now their houses are sinking into the marshy ground. They've been slowly sinking for about twenty years now."

"Why don't they move somewhere else?"

"No one really knows," said Ahab. "But be warned; between here and the marshes, we pass through the 'Dead Village' which is now inhabited only by witches!"

"Witches!" Corliss stopped his horse. "You never said anything about witches, Ahab!"

"No, deliberately. I know how much you fear them."

Corliss stared at Ahab. "Well, in truth, I fear the idea of them. I have never met one in the flesh. But it was the one thing that always scared me most about The Land Beyond, especially when I was a child…"

"Let me ask you something, Corliss. Have you ever considered *why* you fear?"

"You mean; how do I know what fear is?"

"Exactly. If you have never experienced evil and if you have never met a witch, then why are you afraid? Have you never thought perhaps, that the reason you fear these alien feelings, is because you have been here before?"

"Been where?"

"Here, Corliss, The Land Beyond!"

"You're not making sense, Ahab. When have I been here before? As a very small child? I have no recollection of being here."

"Then how do you explain the fact that we know fear when we feel it? How we know anxiety when we feel it?"

"Perhaps because our mothers have been here before, and these feelings are transferred to us in the womb? Energies mixing with other energies."

Ahab thought about that as they slowly started on again. "The only other explanation is that the energies from The Land Beyond, are seeping into our kingdom and affecting us. And if that is the case, then that is a worrying thought."

They travelled in silence now, thinking their own thoughts. Corliss was remembering. As a child he had found a book in his father's library on the subject of witches. These beings existed in The Land Beyond. They dwelled in dark places, places not inhabited by decent folk. And there they wove their web of horror. Witches cast bad spells on innocent people and made sacrifices, often of children. They caused unearthly things to happen, danced around fires and wore strange clothes. It was often said that you could tell a woman was a witch just by looking at her face, as her features would be extremely ugly.

His father had discovered him shaking violently on the marble floor, and the book was open at a page which

114

described the particularly nasty account of a local man who had encountered a group of witches in a wood.

"Why do you have this book?" Corliss had asked his father.

"It is part of the great tapestry of knowledge!" said the king.

But Ahab had a point. Why from such an early age, had he experienced fear? "When will we reach this village?" asked Corliss.

"By sundown," replied Ahab.

As the day drew on and the hour of sundown approached, Corliss could feel his stomach getting tighter. And then, as the sky turned orange, they came in sight of the 'Dead Village'.

They stopped their horses and Corliss turned to Ahab.

"I cannot go in there, Ahab. On my life, I cannot go in there!"

All his limbs trembled now.

"We have to, sire; there is no other way round."

"There must be."

Ahab shook his head.

"I am told that if you stray from the road here…you will never find it again. I would rather take my chances with the witches."

They urged their horses on a bit further until they arrived at the start of what looked like the main street. A sign was hanging on an old wooden post, with the original name of the village. *MARSHWIND,* it read. Apart from the fact that the sign swayed gently in the calm breeze, they could see no other movement. And apart from the fact that the sign creaked on its rusted iron links, they could hear no other sound. The sun sank lower in the sky.

"Let's make a start," said Ahab.

They started to urge the horses forward, but *they* were having none of it. They stamped their hooves and blew loudly through their nostrils. After several minutes of trying, Ahab realised it was no good.

"What do we do now?" asked Corliss.

"We leave the horses here and continue on foot. Who knows, they might be able to find a way round."

"We're going to *walk* through there?"

"We have no other option."

As they entered the village, Ahab drew his knife.

"Keep your wits about you," he said.

The houses on either side of them were tumble- down. The thatch on the roofs had caved in. Old cart-wheels and pieces of cart lay propped against the wall of one house; while a broken chair sat outside the doorway of another. In the middle of the dirt road lay the skeleton of a donkey. Doors were hanging off hinges; debris and decay were the main features of this once quaint little village.

"What happened here?" whispered Corliss.

"Nobody quite knows. But the story goes that nine witches crept into this village one dark night, and with their spells, murdered the entire community and took over the village for themselves. They are the sole inhabitants of this place now. Supposedly, anybody who passes through here is in danger of suffering the same fate as the rest of those villagers."

A terrible shudder made Corliss' body convulse. The worst thing about this place was the silence. It was literally as silent as the grave. No cawing of crows, no sound of wind. Their footfall hardly made a sound either.

Corliss kept glancing through the broken panes of windows, in case a face should be watching them.

In the middle of the main street was a well, long since dried up. Weeds grew between the cracks on the mossy ring of stones.

Suddenly, through the stillness, Corliss heard what he could have sworn was the sound of his own name. His heart leapt into his throat. He spun round. He couldn't work out where it had come from. It was a whispered voice, but even though whispered, it still seemed to have had an echo to it.

"What did you hear?" asked Ahab.

"My own name!" His heart was beating so fast; it almost broke free of his ribcage.

"Someone whispered my name!"

In the next second, Ahab heard *his* name being called. He tightened his grip on the knife handle. Not that a knife would have much chance against nine witches.

"We mean no harm!" shouted Ahab, suddenly. "Let us pass through your domain unscathed!"

An evil laugh, no louder than a breath, alighted on their ears, as if it were a black feather floating on the breeze. The laugh was taken up by other voices. The sound seemed to swirl around those desolate remnants of houses; it came at them from all sides, moving in close and then backing off, as if playing some sort of game.

"They're taunting us," said Ahab. "Is that why you will not come out and show yourselves?"

If he had wanted a reaction to that statement, he got one. *They came;* it seemed, from *everywhere.* One rose up out of the well; two appeared from the shadows, another two clambered out from behind the broken thatch on a roof. And three more clawed themselves up out of the earth before them. Corliss was paralysed with fear.

"That makes eight!" said Ahab, defiantly. "Where is your ninth?"

The ground under their feet suddenly began to tremble violently, as if an earthquake was in progress.

At the far end of the main street, was an old church, crumbling with exposure to the elements. The front door of that church was blown from its hinges with such force that it flew through the air, and in making contact with the ground, splintered into five different pieces.

From that now uncovered doorway, there emerged a woman, draped in a flowing green dress. She drifted serenely towards them, her long dark hair wafting in front of her face.

"You called…*sire!*"

Ahab dropped the knife by his side.

They were surrounded now by the nine witches.

"Ladies," said the witch in green, "we have not had company in such a long time."

They laughed their evil laughs.

"What shall we do with them?"

"Slice them and dice them," said the eight witches, in harmony. *"Boil their toes and rejoice in their woes, as we slowly eat them for dinner."*

"Ladies, please, where are your manners? We have a prince in our midst. Or is that two princes?" She smiled.

Corliss suddenly found his voice.

"Madam, I beg you. We come as friends, and we have no business here…"

"Ah, you may have no business with us, but we might have business with *you.*"

Corliss closed his eyes. He felt weak. His legs buckled underneath him and he fell.

But as he did so, he felt arms catch him. A gentle finger was drawn across his cheek.

He opened his eyes again. The witch in green was before him.

"Master Corliss...your fears are unfounded. Our business with you is benign. You have come a long way. You need rest and food. Welcome to Marshwind, Prince Corliss."

Ten minutes later, Corliss found himself submerged in a tub of hot water, while Ahab reclined in a similar tub beside him.

"Whatever I was expecting," said Corliss, "it's fair to say I was not expecting this!"

Ahab laughed heartily. Above them they saw the sky; the last rays of sun catching the scattered clouds.

When their aching muscles were quite soothed (not to mention their minds), they joined the witches round a large table for dinner. Except that the table was completely bare.

"Prince Corliss," said the witch in green, who had subsequently introduced herself to them as Jessobelle, and was the leader of this pack, "what shall we eat this evening? As our guest, it is your choice."

Corliss smiled.

"A succulent roast pig would be very nice," he said, "but as I have seen no pigs around here, I will settle for anything there is."

"Around here there *is* nothing. But who says we get our food from around here?"

Jessobelle turned and took a burning stick from the fire. She struck the table with it once, and a flame shot out along the length of the table, leaving a trail of fire behind it. The fire leapt up in a bright flare...and on the table in front of them, was a huge roasted pig, surrounded by wine, bread, fruit and three different types of dessert.

Corliss gasped and stared. And then a massive grin spread across his face.

They tucked in, ravenously. And as they ate, the witches told their story.

"Not all nightmares are true, Corliss. You came here this evening with a preconceived idea about witches. But what do people actually know about us?"

"In truth, probably very little."

"People fear what they do not know or understand. But often that fear is not needed. And it gets in the way. We are not what you might call 'black witches'; *they* are few and far between. We are "white" witches, and our powers are used for good, not evil. When we arrived in this village, it was already deserted. We decided to settle here, away from accusing and suspicious locals, but the rumours have circulated ever since, as we knew they would. But we are left largely in peace."

"Why not try and get people to understand you?" asked Corliss. "If they knew what you were really like…"

"We have tried," said Jessobelle.

One of the other witches spoke now. "We have always been outsiders; each one of us. Because of our gifts, our sensitivity, our connection to the elements: EARTH, AIR, FIRE and WATER. We weren't originally witches when we came together, just girls. We were drawn together by our gifts and the fact that we were all shunned by society.

It was then that Jessobelle found us. It was she who began to teach us the art of the white witch. Together we formed a coven and tried to do good with our collective knowledge. But the locals didn't see it that way. They drove us from the town and swore that if we ever came back, they would kill us. We lived in the open for a couple of months before we found this abandoned village. We now call ourselves 'The Marshwind Coven'."

"But there is not much to do good with here, and we are unemployed."

When dinner was over, Corliss took a walk through the village with Jessobelle.

"I am sorry we scared you when you first arrived. We were just teasing. But, we were also testing. We wanted to discover more about you. You are not from around here. You are also very brave."

"No, I'm not," replied Corliss. "Ahab and I come from…" He stopped suddenly. "How do you know our names?"

"That's part of our powers. We know things like that. We've also been expecting you."

"Expecting us; why?"

Jessobelle stopped. She turned and looked at him.

Ahab meanwhile, was being entertained by the other eight; drinking wine and eating bread and goats' cheese, which he had personally requested.

"So you're a prince as well?" asked one.

"It's a complicated story," replied Ahab.

"Nothing is too complicated for us."

"No? Then perhaps," said Ahab, "you could explain something to me?"

"With pleasure."

Ahab paused.

"Why are you all so pretty? I thought witches were supposed to be ugly!"

They all laughed.

Jessobelle and Corliss returned later, to find Ahab asleep on a pile of cushions in front of a roaring fire.

"You must be tired yourself, Corliss. Come, let me show you where you're sleeping."

Corliss lay awake for some time, before finally sleeping. He couldn't help thinking about what Jessobelle had said about them being expected. She knew who they

121

were and she knew they were coming. And then she had told him something else.

"You are in danger, Corliss!"

"What do you mean, danger?"

"Your life is at risk. I cannot tell you why, but I feel it very strongly. I am worried about you, Master Corliss. It is a perilous journey you are undertaking, and I do not know if you will succeed. You are brave, as I said before, but you will need more than bravery in the days to come. I will have to consult the rest of the coven on this one. But I see a picture in my mind of something you will come across. Two old headstones. Whose graves they are I do not know. But they are significant."

Corliss thought this over in his head until he fell asleep.

Ahab found himself awake, suddenly. It was dark and the embers in the fire glowed slightly. He sat up and stretched. A candle was burning and by its light, Ahab became aware of a figure sitting in one of the chairs

"Who's there?" he asked.

"It is I," answered Jessobelle.

"Oh."

"Why are you here?" she asked him.

"I am just passing through on my way to the Great Mountains."

"No!" said Jessobelle. "This village is not on any route to the Great Mountains. Nor any other place for that matter." She paused. "No, Ahab. You came to Marshwind very deliberately, so why?"

Ahab didn't reply at first. He sat in the darkness, feeling the heat from the dying fire on his face.

"There was something I wanted to know. Something I thought you might be able to tell me."

"What is your question?"

"I am following the path of Prince Araznus."

"Yes," said Jessobelle.

"What is my connection with him? Does it go beyond just common feelings?"

"Yes."

"How far beyond?"

Jessobelle did not answer. Ahab repeated his last question.

"I see headstones. That is all."

Ahab didn't look at her; he was afraid to.

"And what can you derive from those headstones?" asked Ahab.

"That one of them has Corliss' name on it. And the other one has yours!"

Jessobelle left him and joined the coven in the old barn away from the house.

"What did you tell him?"

"I told him exactly what I was instructed to tell him; nothing more."

"Do you think Corliss will succeed?"

"That's entirely up to him."

Chapter Eleven

The Fire Spirit

Corliss and Ahab left Marshwind the next morning. Unknown to them, the witches had sheltered the horses in the barn overnight.

As the two of them rode away, Corliss was still thinking about Jessobelle's words. And so was Ahab. Both men had been told what they needed to hear. That was as much as the witches had been required to do. Now it was up to each of them.

Two hours later, they were approaching the marshes and the sinking houses. They could see them, lopsided in the mud, their foundations slowly giving way. A wooden walkway meandered through this bizarre settlement.

A man sat on the roof of his house, which was all that was left of it. He was pulling something up through the chimney with the aid of a long rope. Secured to the roof were several possessions. The man stopped what he was doing when he saw Corliss and Ahab approaching.

"Good morning, sirs. How can I help you?"

"I am Prince Corliss, and this is my friend Ahab. We are travelling to the Great Mountains and require accommodation for the night. Might we find that here?"

"Speak to the village elders; you will find them in the third house on the left."

"Thank you," replied Corliss.

They found the elders in a meeting. The chairs they were sitting on were bolted to the floor, which was at an angle of thirty degrees. They were facing up the slant, where, clinging to a wooden pillar, as though he were quite used to it, was the head elder. "Sorry to interrupt you. We are looking for accommodation."

"I suppose you could say you've come at the right time," said the head elder, as they walked to his house along the raised wooden pier. "As you can see we're holding on to this village by our fingertips. Another fifty years, I don't think it will be here anymore. It's very sad, really. I grew up here. An interesting experience. Some parts of this marsh, you couldn't actually walk on without special splayed shoes."

"Why not just abandon this place now?" asked Corliss.

"Because these are our homes, and provided we can still live in them, we will continue to do so. We have to adapt, accept the situation and make the most of it."

Corliss nodded.

They entered his house; the largest in the village. Stairs led down into a non-existent basement, where now mud came up to the fifth step. Ahab raised his eyebrows.

"I know," said the head elder. "I managed to get everything out. I suppose it makes a rather quirky feature. My spare room is upstairs; follow me."

He led them up to a room under the eaves; pleasantly furnished with a rug over a bare wooden floor, two beds, a chest and oil lamps.

"Here we are."

Ahab stared.

"Do you have another room?"

"Is it not to your satisfaction, sir?" asked the elder.

"We require two rooms…"

"It's fine," said Corliss, butting in. "We'll take the room."

"You can take the room, Corliss. I'm going elsewhere!"

Ahab turned on his heels and marched back down the stairs. The head elder stood awkwardly in the middle of the room, not sure what to do. "I'm so sorry, sir, I…"

"Don't apologise, it was him that was rude. I will take the room, gratefully."

Ahab went back to the other elders. One of them offered him a room in his crooked house and he took it. He was not sleeping in the same room as Corliss. And he wasn't going to pretend anymore. The sooner they got to those graves, the better, as far as he was concerned.

Corliss sat down on one of the beds. He heard Jessobelle's words ringing in his ears, *"You are in danger."* What kind of danger? And from what or from whom? He was in little doubt now. The danger would come from Ahab. It was clear that the friendship was now over. And it was something he would have to confront in due course. In the meantime, Corliss needed some advice.

He set out for a walk on his own and headed towards the woods just in sight of the village. He was looking for an oak tree, and it didn't take him long to find one. He broke off a branch that stuck out of the main bough, then lit a fire. He placed the oak branch in the flames and waited for it to burn. Then left it.

He returned with a lantern when it was dark. He'd taken a tinder box from the house and now began to collect the ash in it. He then relit the fire with new wood, and once he'd got a good flame going, he took a pinch of ash and threw it on the fire.

There was a big flash as the flame flared up and sent sparks flying into the air. But these sparks did not vanish into the darkness; instead they began to dart about like fireflies, and eventually came together to form a gyrating ball of light. And from that light came forth the Fire Spirit.

"Greetings, Prince Corliss. How can I assist you?"

"By telling me straight; is it Ahab I should fear?"

"There are many things that you fear; but none of them you *should"*

"I don't understand."

"Fires can burn you; but I will not. Ahab means you harm, but you should not fear him."

"Why? What have I done to Ahab? And if he means me harm, why should I not fear that?"

"These things you will come to understand in time. I am here when you need me, Corliss."

And with that, the Fire Spirit vanished.

"Riddles. Riddles and more riddles," thought Corliss. Everyone, including Ahab, seemed to have far more knowledge than he ever would, and it was beginning to perplex him.

Chapter Twelve

The Waterfall

Ahab spent an uncomfortable night at an angle and woke the next morning with a sore back. He could almost taste the bitterness in his heart. But he smiled with satisfaction when he thought about the deal he had made with those thieves. Corliss would die, and then he, Ahab, would march back to Amal and claim what was rightly his.

They left the sinking village at nine o'clock. It would take them until mid-afternoon before they reached the graves. Neither of them spoke the entire way; not a single syllable passed between them for five hours.

Corliss felt so dejected. He also felt the fear rising in his chest, despite what the Fire Spirit had told him. It still did not make any sense. How could he *not* be afraid of a threat to his safety? What was he travelling towards? His doom? What waited for him down that long winding road?

It was two o'clock when Ahab suddenly pulled his horse to a stop. Silence fell around them. Apart from a few birds and the distant roar of a waterfall, there was no sound.

For several minutes Ahab sat on his horse and did not move. Eventually Corliss asked, "What are we doing here?"

Ahab now turned to look at him. The expression on his face chilled Corliss to the soul. It was a look of pure hatred.

"What is wrong?" He received no answer. "Ahab?"

Ahab dismounted his horse. He began walking away. "Ahab!"

Corliss jumped down and went after him. He had stopped in front of two large slabs of rock, standing side by side.

As Corliss approached, he realised they were not just ordinary slabs; they were headstones. Why was Ahab looking at headstones? And then, he too, stopped. The air in his lungs froze. Jessobelle had forewarned him of two unknown graves. *This* was what was waiting for him. He turned very slowly away.

"Corliss!" said Ahab, in an icy tone.

Corliss turned back.

"Where do you think *you're* going? I've got a story to tell you."

"You're angry with me. Have I stolen something from you, Ahab? A cow? Berries? Or is this about something much bigger? Something like…title of prince?"

Ahab clenched his fists. His whole body stiffened.

"It wasn't my intention to steal that from you…"

"But you *did,*" grated Ahab between clenched teeth. "You and my father; you stole my birthright!"

"It was a decision that was out of my hands, Ahab, and the title will be returned."

"So you say, but I said I had a story to tell you. It's the story of two men, Araznus and Balthazar. One, a prince, the other an imposter, who *posed* as prince, and took everything the real prince should have had. Araznus was the true prince, Balthazar, the imposter! So what do you think Araznus did about it?"

"He killed his friend?"

"Right. He mowed him down with his horse; trampled him into the ground!"

"So is that what you're going to do to me; kill your best friend?"

"We are *not* friends…"

"But we *were,* Ahab! We've known each other all our lives, and you're going to throw all that away for *this?* It was just a *plan* to see how the other lives; *not* to create a rift *between* us. What do I really have that you don't?"

"You have Mariah! Mariah should be *mine!* I am in love with her! And every day that I see you with her, it makes me mad with rage knowing that she's only with you because she thinks that you're the prince!"

"Then *take* her! Go home and claim her as your own. Tell her the truth and *end* this thing! Because this is not worth losing your friendship over. Our friendship is more important to me than anything. And I am deeply sorry if I have hurt you, Ahab." Tears ran down Corliss' face. "Please; let us reconcile, my friend!"

"It's too late for that! And I am going to make you suffer as I have suffered!"

Corliss dropped to his knees in despair. Ahab went back to the horses and began taking the provisions from Corliss' horse, adding them to his own already laden mare, before mounting her.

"Goodbye, Corliss. May our paths never cross again. I have the only map, so good luck trying to survive on your own out here with no money and no food. Enjoy the rest of your measly little existence…*friend"*

And with that he rode away, past the headstones and on up a slippery track towards the forest.

Corliss tried to call him back, but he could produce no words. His sobs choked him. "Please!" he wanted to say, "Come back; come back and forgive me!"

Suddenly something erupted inside him. He ran after his friend, calling out to him at the top of his lungs. He scrambled up the slope. "Ahab, come back!"

"I will *never* come back for you!" replied Ahab. "We're finished; there's nothing left between us!"

"Please!" yelled Corliss over the sound of the waterfall.

A waterfall! Corliss stopped dead. The roaring filled his ears. He could hear Ahab cursing him.

"The dream!"

The horse and rider had disappeared round a bend. He scrambled after them.

"Ahab wait!"

As he reached the top of the slope, it was right there, huge, awesome and tumbling over the edge with great plumes of white froth plunging down into a mist far below them.

The horse and rider approached the rickety bridge that led to the other side.

"Ahab, you're too heavy! It won't take the weight!"

But the roar was deafening and Ahab did not hear him. He urged the horse onwards.

They were almost halfway across, when the horse's hoof went through a rotten plank.

Ahab looked down. "Corliss...!" he said.

Chapter Thirteen

Back to Reality

The air was balmy.

Jamie stared at Moses as they sat on the steps of the caravan. It was dark now, and Moses had hung two lanterns on the front windows.

"That was the last word Ahab spoke; for at that moment the bridge beneath horse and rider broke, and they were both swallowed up in the raging foam!"

"Now," continued Moses, "that's not the end of the story, but it's late and your parents are going to be worried about you. I suggest you go home, get some sleep, and tomorrow night we'll pick up where we left off. Maybe you could come by about seven. How's that?"

Jamie nodded, sighing, "Okay."

He was reluctant to leave Moses and his tale; reluctant to leave this peaceful environment. Before he left, he asked, "He's on his own, but won't Jessobelle look after him?"

"Perhaps she will," replied Moses.

Ten minutes later, Jamie opened the door to the family caravan. Bob was standing by the sink in the kitchenette with his arms folded. Elaine was doing the dishes. Lauren sat on the couch with her iPhone.

"Where the hell have you been?" snapped Bob.

"For a walk," replied Jamie, calmly.

Lauren sat up straight and took her earplugs out.

"A two hour walk! Rubbish! Tell me the truth."

Lauren waited for his response.

"I was at the arcade for some of the time."

Elaine was still washing the dishes; she didn't even look round.

"You know perfectly well what time your curfew is, young man! Don't ever break it again, understood?"

Jamie nodded but said nothing. He headed for his room and Lauren began to follow.

"Jamie…"

But he closed the door on her.

"What's wrong with that boy!" exclaimed Bob.

Lauren looked at him for a moment, then left the caravan.

She stood outside and took a deep, quivering breath. She started to cry, but she tried to stifle it so that Bob wouldn't hear. She walked a few paces and sat down on a plastic chair. She was so relieved to see him again. When she had returned from the arcade, her head had been swirling with emotion. It had continued to spin ever since. She had barely spoken to her father but she heard him coming outside now.

"Hey, Lauren, you okay?"

She quickly wiped away her tears and composed herself. "I'm fine; I was just worried about Jamie."

"Oh don't worry about that little brat. I'll sort him out good and proper!"

Lauren paused. "And what does that mean?" she asked, not looking at him.

"What does what mean?"

"How are you going to 'sort him out'?"

Bob shrugged.

"I'm going to go to bed now, dad," she said, rising from the chair.

"Sweet dreams, baby girl!"

As she mounted the steps, Lauren did her best not to burst into tears again.

She stepped inside and closed the door behind her. She stared defiantly towards her mother, before going to her room. When she came out again a few minutes later, she was wrapped in her dressing gown. She made two mugs of hot chocolate and took them to Jamie's room.

"Sorry I didn't knock," she said, sticking her head round the door. "Kind of got my hands full." She pushed the door closed with her back. "I made you hot chocolate."

Jamie didn't respond. He was seated on the bed, still fully dressed. Lauren remained quiet. She moved forward and placed the mug down under the lamp.

"Are you okay?" she asked gently. She knew it was a stupid question and he still didn't answer. Lauren sat next to him. She was on tenterhooks; Jamie might yell at her at any moment, and she wanted to try and keep him calm.

"I'm sorry I shouted at you in the fairground." She cradled the mug in her lap. Her brother was staring at the floor. "Jamie, say something to me," she whispered.

Tears began dribbling down her face again. Jamie saw them. Still without saying a word, he reached his hand over and took hers. Together they sat, side by side, and let the hot chocolate go cold.

As Jamie lay in bed that night, his head was full of the story of Corliss and Ahab, and his new-found friend, Moses. He would say nothing of this, however, to anyone. It was for him and him alone; his little secret; something that would give him strength.

134

The next morning at breakfast, Bob was having a go at him again. "You're grounded for the next week. No more little trips out. If you can't obey rules, then you take the consequences."

Jamie looked up at him steadily, "It's my holiday too."

Bob slammed his hand down on the table, making Elaine jump. "Don't answer me back!"

Jamie stood up suddenly, "I'll do what I want."

Bob stared at him. So did Lauren; her stomach was tensing and she'd stopped eating her cereal. "You'll do what I tell you," said Bob menacingly.

"Will I? And what makes you think I'm going to do that?"

'Don't say it', thought Lauren. *'Don't let the cat out of the bag. Because the cat will scratch you.'*

She intervened now. "Dad, let it go. How many times have I broken my curfew? You never grounded me!" Bob dragged his eyes away from Jamie and looked at her. "Just leave it," she said, as calmly as she could.

Elaine stared at the toast in front of her; she wasn't getting involved in this. Jamie turned and left the caravan. Lauren jumped up and ran after her brother.

Bob didn't try to stop him. He sat there, seething with anger. "What the hell is going on around here?" he eventually exclaimed. Then Elaine followed suit, slamming the door behind her. Bob sat there in complete bewilderment.

Lauren chased after Jamie as he walked along the pathway. "Jamie wait!" she called. He didn't stop but she caught up with him. "Jamie, we need to talk…"

"I don't want to talk just now, maybe later."

"But Jamie…"

"No, Lauren."

"I'll play football with you." He didn't answer. "Jamie, look…don't say anything to Bob about…you know, what I told you. It'll just make the situation worse."

Jamie stopped. "It can't get any worse than it is now, Lauren." He continued walking, but Lauren didn't follow.

"I'm here if you want to talk, Jamie." She sighed. "I'll always be here," she said to herself.

Throughout the rest of the day, Jamie thought of nothing but the story, and what was going to happen to Corliss, now that he was alone in The Land Beyond. It was the same as Jamie had felt for years; alone in a harsh land. For the first time in a long while, there was something to comfort him. Like a candle in the dark that didn't flicker. Maybe one day that would be him.

He took himself for a long walk up the hill behind the caravan park, but on the way down he suddenly started feeling wheezy. When he took a puff from his inhaler, he realised that it was out of gas. There was a spare one in the caravan so he would have to go back.

Elaine smiled cheerily as he came in. "Just the person I was looking for," she said. Bob sat on the sofa with a beer in his hand looking annoyed.

"What is it?" asked Jamie.

"I thought we could do something as a family this evening. The fair is still there and we could go to that; play on the rides; get some burgers. What do you think?"

She was plainly making an effort but Jamie stared at her. "Er…I was…I was going to go to the arcade tonight."

Elaine's face fell. "I see." Bob shook his head and took another swig from his beer. "Wouldn't you like to do something as a family?"

"What family?"

"Oi!" yelled Bob. "That's enough of your lip!"

"I wasn't talking to you!" shouted Jamie, spinning round.

"What did you say?" Bob shouted back. He had risen from the sofa. "You watch your mouth. I've put you in your place before and I'll damn well do it again. So just be careful!"

At that moment Lauren walked in.

"What are you going to do? Shove my head in the washing-machine again? Beat me up?"

"Jamie!" shouted Lauren.

"I hate you. I'm not going to spend any more time with this sodding family."

Jamie's face was bright red and Bob's was turning the same shade. He suddenly lunged forward and grabbed Jamie by the scruff and dragged him towards his bedroom.

"Dad, let him go!" shouted Lauren. But Bob shoved him into the room and slammed the door. Then he took a chair and wedged it under the handle.

"You can stay in there, you little brat."

Jamie began hammering on the other side. "Let me out of here" he screamed.

"Shut up!" replied Bob. "We're all going out for a nice evening without you."

"I hate you," shouted Jamie.

"I hate you too!" yelled Bob.

"Dad!" exclaimed Lauren.

"What? You're going to protect him now? He's nothing but a pain in the backside; he always has been."

"Bob…" Elaine began to say.

"I don't want to hear it. We leave him in his room and the rest of us go to the fair. Let's go!"

Lauren picked up her bag and turned to leave.

"Where are you going?"

"The fair! Isn't that what you wanted?

"I thought you were running away."

"Why would I do that? I want to have a nice evening with my parents."

"Is that sarcasm, young lady?"

Lauren just looked at him, before walking out.

Jamie kicked at the door, but it wouldn't budge. He turned away from it and started crying. He had to get out; he had to get back to Moses. He ran to the window but it only opened a little for ventilation and there was no way he could squeeze through. He turned to the door again but it still didn't move and he punched it in anger, then threw himself down on the bed, sobbing into the duvet.

He wanted so desperately to hear the rest of the story. Suddenly, he leapt up and kicked out at the window. With a splintering of glass, it exploded outwards. He pulled his sleeve down over his hand and tried to clear away the jagged pieces that still remained. Then he carefully climbed out, dropped to the ground and started to follow the path that led to the gypsy caravan.

Moses was talking to Mojo as Jamie came walking up. "Good evening, Moses."

The gypsy turned. "So you want to find out what happens to Corliss do you?"

Jamie nodded and smiled.

Lauren tried to make a go of the fair but she was too angry to enjoy herself. She ate the obligatory burger and joined Elaine and Bob for a ride but when they suggested another one, she turned and staggered away sobbing and soon lost them in the crowd. She was utterly desperate.

She hated her father and despised her mother and the only person she cared about now seemed lost to her.

She found a public toilet and went in. With trembling hands, she removed the ecstacy from her pocket and popped all three pills in her mouth, before swallowing them down with water. She needed to blow off steam and try and distract herself. Her jogging gear was in her bag so she headed for the gym.

She started on the treadmill, putting the speed up to a fast jog. After half an hour, sweat was pouring down her face and she felt as if she was burning up, but she didn't stop. And then she fell over.

Chapter Fourteen

Self Defence

Corliss sat on the ground for a long time. He did not move. He stared down into the abyss, into which his friend had vanished.

He was gone, and he was not coming back. Ahab, his companion and lifelong friend, had perished in front of his eyes. And what was more; their last words had been spoken in anger. Was it his fault? Ahab had felt betrayed by him. How long had he harboured these negative feelings towards him? They should never have been told the truth. Ignorance would have prevented this.

From up on a high vantage point, Hanson watched through a telescope.

"There goes the money!" he said.

"At least he's dead!" said Jeremiah.

"There is that. We'll kill the other one, too!"

It must have been an hour later, when Corliss finally roused himself. He didn't know in which direction to go. Should he turn back or continue forward? He found himself wandering along the side of the river, until he found a spot that was relatively easy to cross. He made his way across some stepping-stones to the other side.

He had nothing on him except his clothes and the golden compass the little boy had given him. Slowly he walked back in the direction of the bridge, his head down, his mood so low it was impossible to haul up.

He had no thoughts of the book that lay on the top of that mountain, no thoughts of his father, or even the people of Edomite, who were relying on him so much. His only thoughts were on Ahab. Their whole lives together, up until that terrible moment, replayed itself in his mind.

He remembered playing on the banks of the river together when they were boys; running in and out of the shallows, splashing each other, sunning themselves on the grass. Then they would swim out to a food boat and hitch a ride down river to explore. They would sit amongst the piles of fruit and gorge themselves on strawberries and tell each other jokes.

When Corliss arrived back at the broken bridge, he paused again. "Goodbye, my friend. Forgive me for everything; I will miss you."

And with that he turned and walked into the forest. The path continued upwards, heading further into the foothills. The way was steep and slippery and on several occasions he fell face down in the mixture of mud and loam. He pulled himself up the slope by the aid of tree trunks and finally reached an area where the path flattened out and made the going easier.

An hour later, in the middle of a clearing, he sat down and went no further. What was the point? There was nothing that motivated him to keep going. He lay down in the grass and closed his eyes. He saw the king sitting on his throne; he saw Mariah and he saw Ahab in the main square. At that point he had no idea whether he would ever see Edomite again. He drifted off into a troubled sleep.

He dreamt that men were creeping up on him with knives. Except that it wasn't a dream because men *were* creeping up on him with knives. With a start he sat upright. They surrounded him in a ring. Corliss froze.

"What do you want?"

"A bit of sport!" said Hanson. "My men get bored very easily, you see; I need to keep them entertained."

"And…exactly what kind of sport did you have in mind?"

"Blood sport!" said Hanson.

"How do we play that game?"

"We let you run, and then we chase you! If you manage to get away, congratulations. If not, we kill you! Sound like a good game to you?"

"It certainly sounds fairer than killing me here."

The men backed off, breaking the circle. Corliss stood up.

"You get three minutes to run as hard as you can. Then we come after you. And my men can run fast. Good luck, chum; your time starts now!"

Corliss *ran*! He bolted into the trees, his heart in his mouth. It beat hard and furiously. A strong energy passed through his body. He didn't look back; if these were the last few minutes of his life, he would make them count.

Suddenly he burst out of the trees into a vast open area. It spread out in front of him; the mountains loomed in the distance.

But now Jeremiah came sprinting towards him, a huge dagger in his hand. There was a look of pure determination on his face. Corliss ran like the wind, but Jeremiah was catching up fast. Suddenly Corliss turned and faced his attacker. Jeremiah was not expecting him to stop. He came on in a rush; Corliss stepped aside and clipped Jeremiah's ankle with his foot. He fell forward, hitting the ground hard. The dagger flew out of his hand. Corliss lunged for it. He swiped it up and braced himself for another attack. The rest of them were running towards him now. However, now he had a knife. Jeremiah leaped to his feet.

"Do you know how to use that thing, boy?"

"I'm a quick learner!"

Jeremiah laughed. The rest of them, once again, surrounded him.

"This is not exactly a fair fight, gentlemen! Seven against one; how is that sport? Why don't we drop the knives and just use our hands?"

The men looked at each other; they seemed to like the idea. They sheathed their weapons.

"One on one!" said Jeremiah. "Me first!"

In the middle of the ring, they circled each other. Jeremiah made the first move. He swung a punch at Corliss' head; he dropped to the ground, stunned. He gasped; his vision went fuzzy.

"Get up!" said Jeremiah. "Fight back!"

Tears welled up in Corliss' eyes.

"Just kill me; I have no fight in me. I *cannot* fight! I didn't kill your friend; the man who killed your friend is dead. Do to me what you will; I will not resist."

"You won't fight at all?" asked Hanson. "Do you know nothing of self-preservation? Every man can defend himself." He came into the middle of the circle. "You're right; the man we wanted is dead. You should know, that coward made a deal to save his own skin. He told us to kill you."

"That doesn't surprise me."

Hanson gave him a hand up.

"You'll need to learn how to fight if you're going to survive out here on your own. It's not just us roaming around out here. Let us teach you?"

So what had started as a potentially life-threatening situation, turned into a slightly different one, and Corliss found himself learning hand-to-hand combat and weapon skills.

As the sun began to go down behind the mountains, they were still practising. Corliss was exhausted. At last they stopped.

"Why don't you join with us?" said Hanson. "We are one man short as it is."

Corliss smiled. "Thank you; but that is not possible."

"Ah well; perhaps you will remain with us tonight? I have some business to attend to, but my men will look after you, royally. I wish you luck, Corliss."

The two of them shook hands.

They lit a fire and talked amicably for a while, but then the mood changed.

"So, Corliss; we've taught you how to fight, we've let you sit round our fire and now it's time for something to eat."

"Thank goodness," said Corliss, "I'm starving. What are we eating?"

"You!" replied Jeremiah.

The rest of them laughed. Corliss didn't. Jeremiah was staring at him.

"What do you mean you're going to eat me?"

"We're going to roast you over the fire, like a pig on a spit!"

In the next second, six pairs of arms grabbed him.

"Drag him over the fire, boys!"

Corliss screamed. He struggled wildly, but the men held him tight. In his struggling, something fell out of his pocket; a little tinder box.

"Ah, what do we have here?" asked Jeremiah, picking it up. "Riches?" He opened it. "No," he said, in mock disappointment, "just ash!"

He threw the contents on the fire.

Due to the large quantity of ash, the Fire Spirit now emerged from the flames like a huge fiery demon, towering above them. It was the turn of the men to scream now; like the sparks they scattered in all directions. The Fire Spirit threw balls of blue flame after them.

"You saved my life!" gasped Corliss.

And then with a whoosh, Jessobelle landed next to him.

"Come, Corliss."

He held onto her and they rose into the night sky. They flew up over the treetops, until she set him down again, next to a stream.

"You can rest safe here tonight."

Corliss was silent, but his face said it all.

"I told you this was not going to be easy, Corliss."

"I cannot continue on this quest, Jessobelle. I have not the strength or the will. Tomorrow I will return to my father."

"You need food and sleep, Corliss."

She drew a circle in the dirt. As she did so, he noticed the ring on her finger; silver, with a beautiful green stone. She now blew on the dirt, and another fire sprung up, and next to that, a tray of bread, olives, cheese and wine.

"Think about your future, Corliss. Think about how proud you will feel if you succeed on this quest. How proud you will feel, sitting at your father's side at the great banquet…"

"How do you know these things? What are you not telling me, Jessobelle?"

"I cannot explain."

Before she left, Corliss said, "I like your ring."

Jessobelle smiled. "Rest!" she said.

So Corliss sat alone by the crackling fire and the trickling stream, and got sadder and sadder, the more he thought about Ahab. He didn't touch his food. He would return to Edomite with his tail between his legs; the first prince ever to fail his challenge. He could hear nothing but the running stream and the burning wood.

He thought of a time when he and Ahab went camping together in the grounds of the palace. They had lit a fire and sat round it in the dark, their faces glowing in the flickering light; happy faces, toasting various pieces of delicious food, provided by the palace chef.

They stuck to each other like wet clay; inseparable they were. The palace was their playground; they were always playing hide and seek, and always finding new places to hide.

He wished that was the case now; that Ahab was just playing; that he had found somewhere new to hide, and Corliss just couldn't find him.

He thought again of Mariah. When he returned to Edomite, he would have to tell her the truth about himself and Ahab. Would Mariah ever look at him the same way after that? The man who was responsible for the death of the true prince of Amal. Would she still want to marry him?

It was in the early hours of the morning, when Corliss heard movement in the trees, and a few moments later, a deer walked into the light. The fire was reflected in its eyes. The two of them regarded each other. Corliss sat very still, after remembering what happened with the last deer. He didn't want to scare it. But this deer was different; it seemed very placid. He slowly stretched out his hand towards it. The deer stepped forward and sniffed the air around him. Then proceeded to lie down next to the fire, tucking-in its hooves.

It stayed there until sunrise, keeping him company. Corliss then rose to his feet, picked up the bread and cheese and set off again...towards the Great Mountains.

Chapter Fifteen

The Tree Dwellers

Corliss had been awake all night, thinking not just about Ahab but about his options. He had decided to see how far he could get on his own. He was not doing this for himself, nor for his father, or even the people of Edomite; he was doing this for Ahab. Perhaps somewhere, Ahab would be watching and would be proud of him.

But guilt was driving him as well. He would push himself as hard as he could, put himself through pain, endure the misery and loneliness he would undoubtedly experience; because it was nothing less than he deserved. He had no real idea which direction he was going in anymore. All he knew was that he needed, somehow, to reach the base of Mount Tinprelu. But getting to the top would be a different story. It would be a dangerous, freezing climb to the summit.

His way ahead now lay through a band of thick forest. He walked for hours, not stopping to rest. But at last, overcome by exhaustion, he collapsed at the foot of an enormous tree. He was in a sort of clearing, with a canopy of trees overhead and the sunlight streaming through the branches making patterns on the ground. He could not go another step and he closed his eyes.

When he opened them again, a few minutes later, he got the fright of his life. Suspended, upside down directly in front of him, was a face. But it was a strange face, half covered in hair.

Corliss flung himself away across the ground and sprang to his feet, ready to defend himself. The creature dropped down from the low hanging branch it had been clinging to. It looked half-man, half-monkey and was about five feet tall, with hair covering the majority of its body. It was mimicking every movement Corliss was making. Corliss straightened up, the creature did the same. He narrowed his eyes; so did the creature.

"What are you?" he asked, half to himself.

He was not expecting the creature to reply as it did. "I am a Tree Dweller," it said.

Corliss blinked.

"You looked ill; I came to see if you needed help."

"I need rest. Apart from that…"

"You are sad!"

Corliss stared at the creature for a moment.

"Yes," he said. "I am sad. I lost a good friend."

"Let us help you find him?"

"He's dead!" said Corliss, bluntly.

"Oh; I'm sorry to hear that. Can you climb?"

"Climb what?"

"The trees. We live in the treetops. We can accommodate you there."

Corliss looked up.

"I have no energy to climb."

"Then hold on to me!" said the creature.

Clinging to the Tree Dweller's back, they ascended quickly. The creature was strong and very agile, even with a weight on its back. Up and up and up they went, until they emerged above the tree line…into another world. It was like a city above the ground; rope walks, board walks, tree houses, almost as far as the eye could see. The place was teeming with life.

"Come!" said the creature.

He followed the Tree Dweller along a walkway and into a huge, crowded wooden structure. They meandered their way through the throng, then up a rope ladder to another level, through a further crowded space, up a second rope ladder to a series of individual rooms, with creepers hanging down over the doors. They entered through one.

"Welcome to my abode!" said the creature.

It was a neat little room, with a door at the far end which led out onto a balcony. Halfway up the wall to their right was part of a log, hollowed out in the middle, and stuffed with moss and leaves, to make a cosy bed.

"This place is amazing! How long have you Tree Dwellers been here?"

"Longer than you can imagine," replied the creature. "We have a different view from everybody else. Come and have a look."

The creature led him out onto the balcony. Corliss found himself looking right out to the edge of the forest and beyond, to the eastern range of The Great Mountains in the far distance. It was breath-taking.

"I had no idea," whispered Corliss.

"No idea of what?"

"How beautiful it was. My whole life I've been afraid of this place. The mountains looked terrifying and ominous, and I could only imagine what the rest of it looked like. But I never imagined this."

"We pity the people on the ground. They cannot see beyond their own little lives. They are caught up in their individual affairs. But there is so much more to this world. My name is Indigo; what is yours?"

"Corliss."

"It is a pleasure to meet you. Let me show you to your accommodation."

Indigo took him back the way they had come, where they climbed higher into the branches of a huge tree, to a little hut, nestled amongst the foliage.

"You can stay here!" said Indigo.

This hut had a balcony of its own. When Corliss stepped out onto it, the view to the north caught his eye. Emerging above the tree line, closer than he'd ever seen it, was the summit of Mount Tinprelu.

"Indigo, which is the best route to that mountain?"

"Straight up through the forest; it's maybe another twenty miles. Why?"

"I mean to climb it."

Indigo's eyes widened.

"Climb *that* mountain! You must be mad!"

"I have to."

"That is the highest, most dangerous climb. Many humans have died trying to reach the top. It is a ruthless, un-forgiving peak that will throw everything at you. Ferocious winds, avalanches, sheer walls of ice, ridges as narrow as a knife blade…"

"I do not doubt it; but that is my challenge. Can you help me?"

Indigo sighed, "All right, but you will need special clothing, good equipment…and at least a month of training…"

"I can spare two days!" said Corliss.

"Then we must start at once."

Indigo took him to see someone about climbing gear.

"This is Nabil, and he can provide you with what you need."

"First of all," said Nabil, "you'll need warm clothing, and for that, I will give you this." He produced a thick woolly coat. "This is made from the hair of a mountain sheep, and it will keep you well insulated. Secondly you will need an ice-pick. For that I have just the thing. These are picks that we use when building; it helps us climb when we have wood on our backs. The other thing that helps us are shoes with nails on the bottom. These you will need to give you grip. As for shelter, I can give you a tent made of thick animal hide; this can be folded up easily and placed in a large bag on your back, which will also contain food supplies."

"What about fuel for fires?"

"That is not so easy since no vegetation grows on those slopes; it is all just ice and snow. I will give you some firewood and gloves to protect your hands from the cold."

"What is the easiest way up there?"

"There is no *easy* way up. But I will give you a map, showing you the least dangerous route."

The very next day, Indigo started him on his training. Corliss donned his nailed boots, grasped his pick, and began scaling a section of tree. Indigo climbed alongside him, giving him instructions.

"Not bad," said Indigo, when they were finished. "Your technique is good. Have you climbed before?"

"I used to go rock-climbing with my friend, Ahab. But conditions were better there. This challenge will be very different. Is there anything else I need to watch out for?"

"Mountain lions. They are white, so they're very difficult to spot. They lie in the snow waiting for their prey, usually mountain sheep."

"What do *they* eat?"

"No idea. But mountain lions are ferocious; they will do anything to get their prey."

"How do I defend myself against them?"

"With difficulty!"

Later, Nabil showed him a map of Tinprelu.

"You will come at first to a huge long gully of ice. From there, it is a baptism of fire, for the only way onto the mountain is up a sheer ice-cliff. Once you have scaled that, you're onto the steep slopes. You will have to climb for at least a few hundred feet before you come to a second ice-cliff. There is another route to the east; however, I do not recommend it. It's a very narrow ridge which has claimed many a life. The winds up there can reach eighty miles an hour, and you can easily lose your footing. Beyond that is a field of scree."

"What's above the scree on the eastern slope?"

"Caves, and above that, a very steep ascent to the summit." Nabil sighed. "If you ask me, it is folly; you won't make it!"

Chapter Sixteen

Voices in the Gulley

A day later, Corliss left the Tree Dwellers and began the toughest part of his journey. By late afternoon he was in sight of the gulley. The ground beneath his feet had changed rapidly the further he walked. Now vegetation gave way to rocks and snow.

As soon as he stepped into the ice gulley, he felt the wind. It was a strong, freezing and biting wind. There were no caves in which to set up his tent for the first night. He would have to erect it where he stood. He stuck the poles deep into the ground and hoped the whole thing wouldn't blow away. Once he climbed inside, he was relieved and pleasantly surprised how good a shelter it was against the wind.

Wrapped in his sheepskin coat and gloves, he hunched himself up as small as he could and removed some provisions from his bag, which the Tree Dwellers had sent him away with. They had given him several boxes of dried, cured meat, and lots of chocolate. He also had bread and cheese. He got stuck into the dried meat, which wasn't too bad, thankfully, as that would be his staple diet while he was on the mountain. Once he'd finished his food, he curled up and tried to sleep.

But he couldn't; because that's when the demons came; the dark thoughts that wriggled through his conscious, vulnerable mind. Guilt, sadness, loneliness;

they all filled his head. His argument with Ahab kept replaying itself over and over.

"*You sent me to my death!*" the voice was saying. "*You knew about the waterfall and you did nothing! You're a murderer. You called yourself my friend. But all along you just wanted rid of me; to do away with your competition!*"

"No!" said Corliss. "It's not true; I loved you like a brother…!"

"*Or a servant! That's all I was to you; I packed the horses; I brought you food; I opened all the doors that you walked through! And you call me your brother!*"

"Stop talking to me!" said Corliss, his eyes wet with tears.

And suddenly anger erupted from deep within him. He flung wide the tent and stood out in the open, his arms spread wide. He screamed into the howling elements.

"*Father*; I curse you! What am I doing here? Why should I climb this mountain for you? For a book? It makes no sense!" He looked up into the darkness above him. "Perhaps for a chest of gold or bags of silver; or a gift for Mariah; but not for a *book*! Tell me; what is this about? My friend is dead, I'm on my own out here; do you really expect me to succeed? Oh why am I talking to myself? You can't hear me, no one can!"

"*Corliss!*"

He heard the voice on the wind.

"Speak to me then, whoever you are! Tell me the answers to this riddle!"

"*Ahab has already shown you the path; pursue it.*"

"What path?"

"*Araznus and Balthazar!*"

"What about them?"

"Remember Ahab's words to you. Remember the witches. Think about that and you will move forward along the path!"

"Who are you?" he shouted. "Why should I listen to you?"

"I am the voice that speaks to you from the darkness; the voice of ultimate wisdom. I am your comfort and your reasoning."

"What?"

"I am you!"

And with that the voice faded.

"Me?" said Corliss, frowning.

He crawled back into his tent. The witches; what was it Ahab had said about the witches? And why were Araznus and Balthazar important? He would be able to make no sense of it tonight.

Chapter Seventeen

The Beginning of the Ascent

Corliss swung his pick at the ice. It gouged into it and held. He stuck his nailed boots in and began to climb. It was slow going and the strong wind did not help. Each time he removed the pick, he would have to lean in and hug the wall of ice, then as quickly as possible swing the pick again in order to pull himself up. It was incredibly tiring on his arms and legs.

Up he went; everything above him was white. He tried to think of nothing, just the task in hand. If he thought about what was ahead of him, he would have despaired.

It took him several hours to scale the ice-cliff. He had to rest often, clinging on for dear life, which was not particularly restful. He hadn't dared look down. He kept his eyes on the smooth glistening ice in front of him.

When he finally dragged himself over the edge at the top, he sunk into the deep snow and lay there for a number of minutes, all energy completely drained from his body.

He and Ahab were throwing snowballs at one another. It was mid-winter in Amal, and everything was covered in a powdery white blanket. The sun was shining on their little rosy cheeks.

"I got you, Corliss!" shouted Ahab.

He immediately bent down and began to roll another snowball. Corliss threw one at his back.

"Let's make a snow-angel?" suggested Ahab.

"What is that?"

"It is where you lie in the snow and spread your…"

"No, I mean, what is an angel?"

Ahab stared at him in surprise. "Surely you should know what an angel is, Corliss? It is a being of light that protects and helps you."

"Do they have wings?" asked Corliss.

Ahab nodded.

"I do know about angels," said Corliss, in a quiet voice. "I see one in my dreams. She stands behind me in the room, her hand on my shoulder. She makes me happy."

"What room?" asked Ahab.

Corliss stared up at the sky. The room; that was the other dream. The waterfall and the room with the table. He remembered now; that room had been in his dreams for years. So why were the two coming together now? The waterfall had been real; did that mean that this room really existed as well? And if so, where was it? Had he already been there, or would he go there in the future?

He slowly got to his feet. How could he have known about the waterfall in advance? He had never seen it before. Were the waterfall and the room connected in some way?

He looked up towards the summit; it was a long, long way to go. He began climbing through the thick snow that came up to his knees. His mind turned to Araznus and Balthazar. Ahab had obviously been on their trail; but why? Their story was the same; they were both the subject of a similar plan.

He tried to remember his dream in all its detail. The dreams had all been the same; it was an important room.

Why? What was so important about it? He was always there with other people. It was a meeting. The purpose was to plan something; something to do with Corliss himself.

He climbed for what seemed like hours. The second ice-cliff was getting closer now, but there was no way he was going to be able to climb it immediately.

Suddenly, as he looked up, a huge chunk detached itself from the ice-cliff and came crashing down into the thick snow. The ground beneath his feet trembled violently, and he fell backwards as the whole side of the mountain seemed to cascade down towards him. A fast moving wall of snow was the last thing he saw before everything went black…and silent.

Corliss was out walking in the fields by moonlight. It was a beautiful evening, calm and serene. The sheep bleated softly in the silver light. Corliss was dressed in smart clothes; a stunning tailored jacket and leather boots. He strolled with an air of importance. He had a pipe in his mouth, and the smoke spiralled from it, up over the fields. Silence.

But he was being stalked by a group of six women. They were witches; the most feared in the country, led by the most wicked of them all, Grotchin! Her name alone chilled the blood in even the most hardened of men.

They pounced on him, dragging him to the ground, their nails tearing at his jacket.

"I thought we were having mutton tonight?" said one of them.

"Plans change!" replied Grotchin.

She produced a small slim dagger, the sharp edges flashing in the moonlight. Corliss was screaming.

"Make all the noise you want, little man; no one's going to hear you!"

"We'll start with his fingers," said Grotchin, "they make tasty appetisers. Then we'll cut out his heart. He'll have just enough time to watch it stop beating before he dies!"

Corliss woke, screaming! He was encased in a freezing blackness, snow heavily packed around his body. He could hardly breathe. His fingers were so numb with cold that he could barely feel them. It took him a moment to remember what had happened and to realise where he was. He had been buried by the avalanche. And now he panicked. He frantically cleared an air pocket around him and gulped in breath. How deep had he been buried? He squirmed and wriggled, trying to free himself from the snow. At last he lay, as if in a cocoon. The air was thin, but he was alive.

The witches; it was not just his mind playing games with him; he had been there, in that field. He remembered now. When it was, he had no idea; but it *had* happened. Men had come to his rescue at the last minute; they had axes and wooden spikes and had been hunting the witches for days. They had cut off Grotchin's head with her own dagger, right in front of his eyes. Suddenly he was remembering this all so clearly, as if it had been yesterday. No wonder he had been so afraid of witches.

But then; if he had been scared of witches when he was a boy…? What did this mean?

And it was then that he remembered what Ahab had said to him.

"Don't you feel like you've been here before; in The Land Beyond?"

"Here before?" he muttered. "Before what? Before I was born, you mean?"

"*Yes*!" said Ahab's voice in his head. "*Before you were born!*"

"Who was I, Ahab?"

But Corliss was brought back to the present, by the sound of scratching overhead. He paused and listened. Scratch, scratch, scratch.

"Is that somebody there?" shouted Corliss.

Scratch, scratch, scratch.

"Help me!" he called.

The noise was getting closer.

"I'm down here!"

The snow above him now began to break away and something emerged through it; a wet shiny nose. Corliss laughed. Somebody had arrived with a dog to save him. He reached up and tickled the snout that was beginning to show itself. As soon as he did this, the snout opened wide to reveal a row of huge, sharp, glistening teeth and a massive red tongue. A second later the mountain lion shoved its head into the hole. Corliss screamed! The lion roared, then snapped its jaws, narrowly missing his arm. Corliss flattened himself against the compact snow as the lion snapped again. He swung his fist at its snout again and again; the lion roared angrily. Saliva dripped from its teeth.

The ice-pick, where was it? Corliss frantically began feeling about in the snow for it. If he didn't find it, he would surely die; he had a matter of minutes. He dug himself deeper into the snow now; it was the only thing he could think of. The snow gave way quite easily; he burrowed further in, his heart pounding with fear. The lion still only had its head poking through, as if it couldn't get in. Corliss dug faster.

And then with a shove, the lion *was* in. Its teeth clamped around his ankle. Corliss grasped at the snow in front of him and tore away a huge chunk. And suddenly he saw it; sticking out towards him, the handle of the ice-pick. Corliss grabbed it just as he was dragged backwards. The lion was pulling him out of the hole. He let himself be dragged. He could feel the air now. As soon as he was out, just as the lion opened its jaws to kill him, he rolled over onto his back and swung his ice-pick.

The great beast crashed down on top of him, its blood staining the white snow. Corliss lay for several minutes, breathing heavily. At last he struggled free from beneath the animal.

He took the already bloodied pick and ripped open the lion's belly. He shoved his freezing hands inside the carcass; it was gloriously hot. A contented laugh gurgled up in his throat; he was alive, and he was warm. The steam from the animal's stomach billowed around him in the cold air, bathing him in droplets of heat.

Two hours later, he sat outside his tent with a large piece of lion meat roasting over a fire. There was plenty more where that came from; it was a big animal. It would keep in the cold temperature and he could take the chunks of meat with him up the mountain.

He had moved off the main slope, out of the path of the avalanche. And this was now his route; the first plan would have to be revised. He *was* going to have to take the ridge, and he was not looking forward to it; as Nabil had said, several people had perished trying to attempt it. But then what were his odds anyway; not brilliant. Yes, he had survived the avalanche, and escaped the jaws of a mountain lion; but what other challenges would this mountain throw at him? He still had a long way to go.

He sat in the shelter of his tent and felt the heat from the fire. The sparks rose into the night sky. He wished he had the ash to scatter on the flames; he needed someone to talk to. He chewed on the hot meat.

It had started to snow now; large flakes began to swirl around him and soon it turned into a blizzard. He crawled further into his tent.

"Hello!"

Corliss stuck his head out.

"Hello?" he asked.

The voice was soft and whispery.

"How can I help?" it asked.

"Where are you? *Who* are you?"

"I am an Ice Spirit! I am here for you, Corliss. Tell me what is on your mind?"

"I want to know the truth; I want to know who I was, who I *am*? Ahab was following in the footsteps of Araznus and Balthazar. But are those footsteps *our* footsteps? Are we one and the same?"

"Yes!" whispered the Ice Spirit.

"But how is that possible?"

"The universe is a complex system; you have many different personalities; they come and go; they leave their mark; they inspire others. Ahab and you have collided before, as Araznus and Balthazar. You are doing it again in this time."

"But Balthazar died; and now Ahab has, too. What is death? What does it mean?"

"Death is an in-between period. Ahab is lost to this world, but perhaps you will see him again in another existence."

"So where is Ahab now?"

"*Who can tell?*" said the Ice Spirit. "*Perhaps he is in a faraway place that cannot be reached by the physical form? Or perhaps he walks with you still? The answers you seek are out there, Corliss; you will find them, you just have to keep looking.*"

"Why can *you* not tell me?"

"*You have to find out for yourself; that is the way it works. I can only tell you part of it; you must continue on your quest to find out the remainder of the puzzle!*"

"What is in that book?" shouted Corliss.

But the Ice Spirit had departed.

*   *   *   *

Jamie stretched. "I like these different spirits he talks to, especially the Fire and Ice spirits. It would be great if you could call up a spirit to give you advice; in reality, I mean."

"Some people say you can. Like my mother, for example. She used to tell me that everyone has a spirit guide who is assigned to them during their lifetime. Those who are sensitive enough can hear this guide. My mother had two guides and that's how she got a lot of her information."

Jamie grinned. "Cool," he said.

Moses laughed.

"In my mind," continued Jamie, "I have an owl. I created him as a relaxation technique, but sometimes I feel that he wants to tell me something, like he's really there, not just part of my imagination."

Moses frowned. "That's interesting. Perhaps you should try listening."

Jamie nodded. "In The Land Beyond there seem to be different types of inhabitants. On one hand you've got normal human beings and on the other you've got creatures like the Tree Dwellers. Why is this?"

"The world has many different types of people. The Tree Dwellers represent people who have their own gifts and think differently from others. These people have their own view of the world; their own perspective. This is represented in the story by the idea that they've developed their own skills and their own features. Not only that but their separateness allows them to have a unique view of the world and all its beauty; aspects of which are unknown to what we might call 'normal' human beings."

"Corliss says to Indigo that he didn't realise how beautiful The Land Beyond was. He thought it was grim."

"Yes. It is fear of the unknown. His ideas of this other world were tainted by fear. But, as Jessobelle said, our fears are often unfounded."

"And what about my anxieties and sadness? Are you going to tell me that they are unfounded too?"

"For you, they are not; but your soul knows differently."

"My soul?"

"The other part that drives you; the apple tree."

*　　*　　*　　*

Lauren lay on the floor of the gym, her face bright red, sweat dripping off her body.

The attendant was doing CPR, when the manager rushed in.

"What's going on?"

"She just collapsed! One minute she was pumping iron, and the next minute she was on the ground!"

"Call an ambulance!"

"I already have; they're on their way. She's really burning up here!"

The manager noticed the locker key that was clipped to her leggings. He took it off and went to the changing rooms, which were now empty. It was half past nine.

He examined her clothes, looking for any signs of identity. He found a bus pass in her jeans pocket. She was a minor; he had to find the parents. Easy enough; just compare the name against the register to find out which plot she was in.

Bob opened the door to the manager's knock.

"Good evening, Mr Fairweather. Do you have a daughter by the name of Lauren?"

"Yes!" said Bob, alarmed. "What's wrong?"

Elaine came out of the master bedroom, wrapped in a dressing gown.

"Who is it?" she asked.

"Sir, your daughter has collapsed in the gym; an ambulance is on its way."

Elaine went berserk.

Five minutes later she was scrambling into the back of the ambulance with her daughter.

"I'll see if I can find Jamie!" said Bob.

As the ambulance pulled away, Bob put a hand to his head and started to cry. He sat down on a plastic chair.

"My baby!" he kept saying. "My baby!"

In the ambulance they took a blood sample from Lauren.

"What's that for?" asked Elaine.

"We need to see what's in her system; helps us to find out what's wrong with her. When was the last time you saw your daughter?"

"About an hour ago," replied Elaine.

She wiped her eyes and stared at her daughter's face. She looked peaceful.

They arrived at the hospital and transferred Lauren to A&E where she was seen immediately. Half an hour later, the blood results came back. A doctor came to speak to Elaine, who was seated in the waiting area with a cup of tea out of a machine.

"Mrs Fairweather, your daughter has high levels of the drug ecstasy in her blood."

Elaine stared at him in horror.

"What?"

The doctor nodded.

"Ecstasy is one of the most dangerous drugs out there and can cause permanent brain damage. We're going to do a CAT scan to see what the situation is."

Elaine's hand began to tremble.

"How the hell did she get hold of it?"

"Unfortunately, that's the easy part. Ecstasy is a very common drug, very popular among teenagers. She could have got it at a party or through a friend."

"How is she?"

"At the moment she's still unconscious and showing no signs of response."

Elaine closed her eyes.

"The other thing we're concerned about at the moment are her liver and kidneys. She collapsed, I believe, in the gym. What tends to happen with ecstasy, is it overheats the body, especially when it's active. And this can cause damage to these particular organs."

Elaine broke down in tears.

"Can I see her?"

"Of course!" replied the doctor.

Lauren was lying in the intensive care ward with a breathing tube down her throat and a monitor next to her. Elaine pulled up a chair to her bedside, as the doctor drew the curtain around them. "I'll be back in fifteen minutes to take her for a scan."

Elaine touched her daughter's face.

"Sweetheart, it's Mum. I'm here, and I'm not leaving you. You're going to be alright. Everything's going to be alright. I poured away that whisky. I didn't take a drop. Not anymore, baby. Not anymore. I know this is all my fault. Mine and no one else's. *I'm* the alcoholic; I had the affair. Your dad may not be the most intelligent man alive, but he loves you. I love you more than anything else in the world. You and your brother are the most wonderful things in my life. Because I created you. That makes me very proud, it's the best thing I've ever done; having children; although I'm a lousy mother; a lousy wife; not to mention a lousy stripper."

Elaine started to cry again. "But if you give me another chance; I promise I'll do my damnedest to be a better mum! I'll go back to rehab, I'll kick this habit right now. I'll listen to you; both! I'll watch you guys grow up and go to college. Come back to me, my darling. Don't go where I can't follow!"

Chapter Eighteen

The Ridge

Corliss walked for miles the next day. He climbed higher and higher towards the ridge; and the further he went the colder it became and the stronger the wind blew. It took him several hours to reach the top. The slope was almost vertical and he had had to use his pick most of the way.

Nabil was right; the ridge was as narrow as a knife blade. A very thin, rocky path was all that stood between him and certain death right on either side. He struggled to keep his balance. Several times he almost toppled over the edge. He realised that the only way to do this was to crawl along on his belly. He flattened himself to the ground as the wind rushed over him. Soon another blizzard blew up and he could see nothing at all. He clung to the ridge and didn't move. If the weather carried on like this, he would surely freeze. His face and body were numb with cold. Carefully he inched his way forward; he had to keep going; he had to.

He thought about the markets in Edomite, selling ice. He used to love going there on a hot day and surrounding himself with these large, freezing stacks of frozen water from the mountain glaciers. Smooth, wet, glistening blocks under the canopies, dripping in the heat. He would watch the men carving out chunks for individual usage.

He remembered, too, swimming in the rivers that came down from those mountains; bathing in the deep pools of cool water; sitting on the rocks underneath the waterfall.

He wished he was back there; that all of this was just a dream, and he would wake up in his bed in the palace. And he imagined Mariah coming to greet him. He had hardly given her a moment's thought over the past week or two; his mind had been on very different things.

If it was true that he had many personalities and many lives; then why was he here now, scaling this vast mountain? For what purpose had Ahab died? It seemed like there was neither rhyme nor reason to it. And yet, he had known about the waterfall and Ahab's potential death. Could he have done more to prevent it? Was Ahab right; was he a murderer? A murderer and a thief! Was he getting even with Ahab from their previous lives as Araznus and Balthazar? What *was* the story behind those two men?

He crawled steadily onwards; the whirling snow blinded him.

Corliss had a blindfold over his eyes; he was in the middle of a circle of boys in the palace ballroom; they were walking round him; it was a game; he felt his way forward, trying to catch one of them, but they backed away. They were creeping on tiptoes, so that he couldn't hear them; the object was to try and use the other senses, to pinpoint where they were by listening for the slightest creak on the floor or a very quiet breath.

Corliss could hear nothing now, but the howling wind. He had no concept of time as he clung to that ridge for dear life; he made slow progress. The blizzard continued for what was possibly hours. At last it cleared. He saw the sky again and the great peak; he looked back and saw that he had come quite far. Gingerly he peered over to his right; the ridge dropped away, three hundred feet beneath him; below that he could see the pine trees of the forest; from that height they were like little saplings.

Ahead of him the ridge ascended higher. He wasn't going to make it; the way ahead looked like the scaly back of some monster; uneven and treacherous. The storm had deposited a large amount of snow; another was approaching and he heard the rumble of thunder and the flicker of lightning. The clouds were black and menacing.

Ten minutes later he was surrounded by a downpour of torrential rain; it lashed against his face; forks of lightning flickered wildly in the clouds. Corliss' muscles were racked with pain, but his skin had no feeling at all. He clung on tight. He had to get off this ridge, it was not safe. But he was petrified and as much as he wanted to get off, he didn't dare move.

He deserved this; this was his punishment for what he had done to his best friend.

"I love you, Ahab; our friendship was everything. Remember the plays we used to perform? You would play the prince, and I, your servant. Well if you were jealous once, then look at me now! Vulnerable, afraid, alone; I wish you were here, Ahab. I would tell you how sorry I was. Because it is all nonsense; it does not matter anymore who is prince and who is not; you are dead and I am in torment. I have nothing, Ahab; I am a humble citizen of Edomite. Mariah is in love with an idea; that idea being that I am prince. Why should she love *me*, Corliss, the servant? Take away my title of prince and I am nobody. There is something that I am not seeing; it is bigger than all of us, bigger than the roles we are playing."

At that moment a huge fork of lightning struck the rocks in front of him and the path disintegrated. He toppled sideways and out into thin air; and here he plummeted downwards through the storm, down towards the forest.

If he had been unaware of time before this point, he now became acutely aware; it had slowed, considerably. Everything was now so calm and peaceful; there was no fear of death or pain, just a great sense of letting go. Nothing mattered anymore.

He saw Ahab laughing, good humouredly; he saw Mariah smiling at him. He saw the concert hall with its stunning diamond ceiling. Lightning flickered. He heard his last words; *it is bigger than all of us, bigger than the roles we are playing.*

Suddenly, in that flash of light, he got a glimpse of what it all meant; he saw the pages of the book being turned; he saw the room with the angel; he saw a hooded figure; and he saw himself.

Jessobelle caught him as he fell fast towards the ground; she swooped him back up into the sky, back up towards the mountain. But she did not set him down there; instead she set him down beyond it, in the middle of the scree and boulders. Here he was safe. She slipped something into his pocket, and then she was gone again, into the night.

When Corliss woke a few minutes later, he had no idea where he was. He even thought that he might be dead. He rolled over because a stone was digging into his shoulder, and sat up. He was leaning against a huge rock but it took him a while to work out that he was still alive.

He couldn't believe he had survived the fall. He pulled himself to his feet; when he turned around, he saw the ridge beneath him. He blinked and stared; it wasn't possible; he had fallen. He looked up towards the summit. The wind and rain had ceased; high up above the mountain top, he saw the moon, bigger than he'd ever seen it before; it illuminated the summit; it shone on the frozen river that had once meandered down from the lake. It was like looking at the pathway, the pathway that would lead him to the truth. And he realised now that the truth lay within the pages of that book that his father wanted him to get. And nothing was going to stop him from getting it. From now on there would be no more listening to disembodied voices. He knew what he had to do.

Chapter Nineteen

The Caves

Corliss looked at the map; according to this, the caves should be somewhere close above him. As he climbed over boulders and mounds of little stones, he couldn't help but wonder how he came to be up here. But he suddenly became aware of something digging into his right leg. He placed his hand in his pocket and removed a small object; a ring with a green stone set into it. Jessobelle's ring! He smiled; then he slipped it on his finger, and continued to climb.

He reached the cave entrance a short while later, and with grateful joy, entered the dry, sheltered space. He didn't even bother making himself comfortable; he took off his bag, flopped onto the ground and went to sleep.

He awoke a few hours later, a little cold. He sat up; everything around him was pitch black. He fumbled in his bag for a piece of wood and managed to get it lit. Then, using that as a torch, he ventured further into the cave.

It seemed to be of a considerable size; the ceilings were tall and the further back he went; he began to see bats clinging to the rock above him; huge numbers of them. How old was this place, he asked himself? What secrets did it hide? The bats were shifting about now and he tiptoed quietly so as not to disturb them. He came across strange carvings in the rock. He was wary about going too far in; but just as he was about to turn back, he heard the sound of rushing water. He had to find the source. He rounded a bend in the cave; and almost fell into a lake. On the other side, water was pouring down into it, through a hole in the rock wall. Corliss stared at it; that water had to be coming from somewhere. He skirted the edge of the lake to get a closer look. He peered up through the large hole through which the water was gushing. Was there a way up there? And was it an easier and safer climb than the edge of the mountain? Instead of climbing up the outside, why not climb it from the inside?

He went back to get his bag and returned a few minutes later. He stuck the burning torch into the top of his bag, slung the bag on is back and started to climb the waterfall. The inevitable happened; he was deluged with water and the torch went out almost immediately. He was clinging to the slippery stone one minute, and the next minute, lost his grip and fell. He landed on his bag, soaking wet and irritated. He slapped his hand down angrily.

At once a bright, white light illuminated everything around him. For a moment he was dazzled; he shielded his eyes. As he raised his hand, the light moved with it. And then he realised the source of the light was the stone in Jessobelle's ring.

"I didn't know it could do that!" he marvelled.

His voice echoed.

Corliss scrambled up through the waterfall with the aid of his ice pick. The water was freezing; it poured into his collar, running down his back, giving him a sense of cold he had never felt before, not even on the frozen slopes. He didn't care anymore; there was a determination in him now that drove him forward with a passion. He had to complete this task; he had come this far.

He climbed for twenty minutes until he reached a shelf, with a large recess. He clambered onto it, dripping wet, and collapsed onto the smooth, dry stone, breathing heavily. Ahead of him, another narrow shelf sloped up to run parallel to the gushing water, which might mean he could still follow it without getting wet. He would investigate tomorrow; it was now late into the night and he needed more sleep.

He opened his bag now to discover a slushy mess; everything was sopping wet. The slabs of meat he had wrapped in some cloth were the only things still edible; if only he could find some dry wood. Once again he was freezing cold and he needed a fire quickly. He pulled off his wet things, which weren't helping and rubbed his skin furiously. What on earth was he going to do? He was hunched, naked, in the middle of a dark cave. He tried fiddling with the ring to see if it would produce a fire as well as a light, but nothing happened. His skin was covered in goose-bumps and he wasn't sure if he could bear this cold any longer. He started blowing on his hands.

And as he did so, he blew on the ring. Heat began to emanate from the stone; a heat so powerful that he felt its rays immediately. Soon he was basking in a warm glow; the cold had gone completely. He laid out his wet clothes and proceeded to dry them. It took half an hour for them to fully dry.

He was very hungry, but there would be nothing more for him to eat tonight.

The next morning, he set off again up the narrow ledge. He walked for hours; the cave was low and he had to stoop the entire way; his back was aching.

At last he saw a wide opening ahead, and a minute later he emerged into an enormous cavern, the like of which he had never seen. He stopped dead, staring in amazement.

In front of him stretched another huge lake, bigger than the first one. The ceiling of this cavern was as high as a ten-storey building. And hanging from that ceiling were hundreds of stalactites as big as swords; all around him on the ground, were hundreds more stalagmites. Corliss didn't move for a long time. He took his bag from his back and laid it down. He walked forward towards the lake and peered into its depths.

But as he looked, the face that was reflected back at him was not his own face, but someone entirely different. Corliss quickly drew away, his heart thudding wildly. He touched his cheeks; then very gingerly took another look. This time they were his own features that were reflected there. He must have imagined it; or else the surface of the water had distorted what he saw. He dipped his fingers into the water, then cupped his hands and splashed his face. The water was not cold, but tepid, like a bath that had lingered too long. There was something about this lake that was different from others.

Corliss removed his clothes and waded into the shallows. He walked in until the water came up to his waist, then he began to swim. He swam out into the middle; and there he treaded water, waiting for…something.

"What am I waiting for?" he demanded, out loud.

Suddenly, in the water beneath him, light began to sparkle and dance, like a luminous, swirling current. It swarmed around his legs, moving up his body until it bubbled right up to the surface. And as it touched his chest, his heart began to beat faster and images flashed into his mind.

Everything seemed to open up and become crystal clear; he knew who he had been; he knew his name, his thoughts, his feelings; he was that person again, that person who had stared back at him from the reflective surface of the lake. He could hardly believe it, but it made total sense.

When the lights finally died away, down into the depths, he felt a strength in him, he had never felt before. He frolicked about in the lake like he was a child again. He screamed out with joy, listening to his voice echo around the cave.

Corliss dried himself with the heat from the ring and put his clothes back on. He was suddenly so hungry he could have eaten an entire table full of food. He'd ditched the old food, which was now inedible; the only thing he had left that was still salvageable was the slab of meat he had cut from the lion. He placed it on a stone and began trying to cook it, by focusing the ring's heat. He sat for an hour, waiting for the meat to cook. At last he began to smell the aroma, as the meat started to sizzle gloriously on the stone.

But the smell of that cooked meat had wafted, and mountain lions can pick up the scent of a goat days after it has passed. So the smell of roasting flesh was not difficult for them to detect. They had followed their noses and found their way into the cave. Eight of them now came across Corliss, sitting with his back to them; it was too easy.

But at that moment, one of them stood on a stalagmite and broke it. The noise made Corliss spin round. He took one look at those monsters and swiped up his pick; but there was no way he could fend off that many. He made a dash for the lake and dived in; he swam out as far as he could go, then turned to look.

The lions were watching him, their eyes black and cold. For a while, they simply stood looking at him; then the largest beast in the pack, moved towards the edge of the water. It dipped its paw in, almost as if it was testing the temperature. And then, very calmly, it entered the lake and began to swim strongly and confidently out towards him.

Chapter Twenty

Life or Death

Corliss' heart almost stopped beating. He hadn't thought that perhaps they could swim, too. The lion was getting closer and he began to panic. Suddenly he took a deep breath and dived down under the water. He watched the lion, to see what it would do now. Its face peered under the surface for a few seconds, before it started to dive. Corliss screamed, even under the water, which gushed into his mouth; he closed it abruptly and swallowed. His lungs were bursting; the lion was swimming down towards him.

Corliss suddenly did something he did not think he could do; he swam towards the oncoming threat, brandishing his pick. He swung it through the water; but with one clean swipe of his enormous paw, the lion knocked it out of his grasp. Now the claws came out, the teeth were bared and the tiger grappled with him. The claws tore at his flesh; extreme pain shot through him; he was fighting this enormous beast with nothing but his bare hands. His lungs were crying out for air; the lion had the advantage.

And then, all of a sudden, it broke away from the attack and swam back to the surface; even lions need air. Corliss did the same; he emerged from under the water, spluttering and coughing, gasping for breath. The lion could see him, but it did nothing to re-engage him. Instead it headed back to the shore. It scrambled out onto the rocks and slunk back to the other lions.

Corliss continued to tread water; he had to come up with a plan. Or did he; maybe they would just give up now. The first lion had tried and failed; would that be the end of it?

Unfortunately, not; the lions began to position themselves around the side of the lake; all eight of them; and then all eight entered the water. Corliss took several deep breaths and again dived under the surface. He swam down and down, trying to draw the lions as deep as possible. When he glanced back, he could see them all following. He hit the ring with his hand and the light sprang out of the stone, illuminating the bottom of the lake; he had to locate his pick. He saw it, lying in amongst the weeds. He retrieved it now; but at that moment, the ring slipped off his finger; he grabbed hold of it, just as it floated away and instinctively put it in his mouth and clamped it between his teeth, with the stone facing outwards, so he could still see where he was going.

It was not immediately apparent to him, and it took a few moments for him to realise that he was breathing. He removed the ring from his mouth, and immediately noticed the difference. He replaced it in exactly the same fashion, his teeth clamping down on the silver band, and once again he could breathe. This truly was a remarkable ring: combined within it seemed to be all the tools he needed to survive.

Now it was he who had the advantage. The lions were gaining on him but then he saw it; a hole in the rock. It was big enough for him to hide in, but too small for the lions to gain access. He made for it and concealed himself inside.

As soon as he did, he realised it was a tunnel; but where did it go, and was it safe? It was very narrow and dark, and flooded with water. It was possibly his only way out of these caves now; the lions would wait for him. He began to half-swim, half-wriggle his way through the tiny space. The walls were covered in some sort of slimy weed. He hoped this would not suddenly stop; he didn't relish the idea of having to try and swim backwards.

He didn't know how long he was in that tunnel for; was he the first to explore it? Finally, the tunnel began to get wider and he found himself in a small pool. When he surfaced, he was in another cave, but considerably smaller than the one he had just come from. He dragged himself out and looked around him. There was another tunnel to his left.

The ring illuminated something, tucked into the back of this cave…a series of wooden boxes. Boxes; somebody *had* been here before. When he went to examine them, he found a piece of parchment on the top of one. It read, simply, *FOR THOSE WHO PASS THIS WAY! PLEASE ENJOY THESE GIFTS!* When Corliss opened the first box, he could hardly believe his eyes; it was brimming with food. And so was the next and the next. The last box he opened contained piles of dry wood. He shrieked with joy and hastily began unpacking.

Half an hour later he sat on the cave floor in front of a roaring fire, devouring roast chicken, potatoes, wine, bread and cheese. It felt so good to be rested and fed at last. He almost felt like he deserved it. He was warm, dry and as far as he knew, safe.

He spent the night there and the next morning, after eating a hearty breakfast, packed up as much food and wood as he could stuff into a bag and set off up the next tunnel.

When he finally came out into the light again, it was almost blinding against the white snow. He shielded his eyes and breathed in the fresh air. As his eyes became accustomed to the light and he made out the view, it was astoundingly beautiful. From where Corliss stood he could see the tops of the mountains poking up above a fluffy layer of cloud. He realised just how high up he was and he looked up towards the summit once again. What other challenges awaited him?

Chapter Twenty-One

The Final Ascent

Corliss now found himself clambering up through the scree field, Nabil had told him about. The ground under foot was a layer of loose stones that shifted constantly as he walked, and dotted about him were massive boulders. How exactly they had come to be there, he could only imagine. And how long had they been there? Years, centuries, millennia?

It took him half a day to climb through the scree field. Once he'd done that, he reached the frozen waterfall that would take him onto the frozen river; and from there, there was only one more gruelling climb to the top.

It took him another half day to get to the summit. As he reached it, the sun was low in the western sky. He stood, watching it slowly sink behind the mountains. He had done it; he had reached his destination. A sudden wave of emotion passed over him; tears streamed from his eyes. He flopped onto his knees, his chest and shoulders heaving. It had taken him almost a week to scale this vast mountain, and he had done it all on his own. He had not thought it possible; he had assumed that he would die in the attempt; and he almost had.

But now he was on the plateau at the very top of Mount Tinprelu, looking towards another lake and green foliage on the far shore. It was as if this plateau had a climate of its own; temperate and forgiving; as if this was the mountain's reward to those who could conquer her. And in amongst that foliage, Corliss saw the roof of a wooden hut.

The door gave a slight creak as he pushed it open. The interior was small and basic; a low ceiling, and a wooden table and chair. And in the middle of that table…was a large, leather-bound book with gold leaf.

Corliss stared at it without moving. There it is, he thought; this is what I have struggled for; this is what I lost my friend to achieve. He stiffened suddenly, in anger. He had a strong urge to walk away from it now, to leave it where it lay; to defy his father. Whatever was in that book, whatever truths lay hidden within its pages, those truths could not give him what he wanted more than anything; they could not bring Ahab back to him.

He turned and left the hut, walking away through the bushes. He climbed up onto a big rock and sat looking towards the orange sky that silhouetted the jagged peaks of the Great Mountains.

"I've done it, Ahab; what do I do now?"

It was almost as if he were actually waiting for an answer. Where would it come from, he wondered; on the air, like the voices in the gully, or from inside him? Would he just know, instinctively? He thought about what he knew already, what the lake in the caves had told him – that he was Araznus. He still needed to digest that knowledge properly; it was almost too much for him to take in right now.

After watching the sky turn darker and no answer appearing, he returned to the hut. He lay down on the floor, closed his eyes and tried to sleep; but sleep did not come. He opened his eyes and lay there in the darkness, listening to the absolute stillness. He should have been happy and glad that he had done what he had set out to do; he should have been proud that he had accomplished his father's task. But he felt neither of those things. In fact, there was no emotion at all. He drew light from the ring, sat on the chair and stared at the book.

It didn't look like anything extraordinary; he had seen plenty of books like that in his father's vast library. It was just a simple book…that could be burnt like any other; and that's what he wanted to do with it now; destroy it! But somehow, he couldn't bring himself to do that. It wasn't because his father would be angry with him; it wasn't because he would fail his challenge; it was just that…it wasn't an option.

He sat up half the night, as if he were taking the time to get to know this leather-bound object that had been the cause of all his hardships over the past few weeks. By the time he finally tried to go back to sleep, he had traced every tiny millimetre with his eyes; run his fingers and his palms over it many times and had got to know the smell of it. It smelt old; as if it had sat in a mouldy attic for centuries, just waiting to be read.

When he woke early the next morning, he opened the front door to a beautiful sunrise. The sun shone on him that morning as though he were the only person in the world. It was just Corliss and the sun, greeting each other on the dawn of a new day. He went to bathe in the lake. It felt so invigorating, so fresh; like the first bath he had ever taken.

Corliss packed the book into his bag as if it were no more than a piece of wood. He would give it barely any thought until he reached Edomite.

Chapter Twenty-Two

A Bittersweet Return

It took him less time to descend the mountain than it did to climb it. As he walked, he felt strangely at peace. A calmness had settled over him that he hadn't felt for a while. He took in the beauty around him; pausing to gaze at particularly stunning views. It was as beautiful as Amal, and yet at the same time it was different. He was realising finally that despite all the fear and anxiety, The Land Beyond was a fascinating place with many different moods.

Three days after leaving the mountain behind, Corliss was walking along the road towards Amal, when a voice stopped him in his tracks.

"Do you still have my ring?"

Corliss smiled and turned. She was standing by the roadside in her green dress.

"I do!" he replied, slipping it off his finger.

"Thank you," she said.

"Thank *you*!" Corliss looked at her steadily. "You saved my life!"

Jessobelle nodded.

"Why?"

"I think you know why."

Corliss smiled again.

"You wanted to make amends. After all, you almost killed me in that field; if those men hadn't shown up...But maybe you should have; I wouldn't have killed Balthazar if that were the case."

Her eyes brightened.

"You swam in the Lake of Knowledge then?"

"I did. But I never imagined that…"

"That you were Araznus?"

Corliss nodded.

"I still don't understand."

"The book will fill in the gaps."

"Ah yes; the book. I'd almost forgotten it was there. Is there anything I can do for you in return?"

She smiled, a little sadly, it seemed. "No; there is nothing you can do for me. I'll be fine; we'll be fine."

"At any rate, allow me to try?"

Jessobelle raised an eyebrow questioningly.

"What do you have in mind?"

Two days later Corliss and the Marshwind Witches walked purposefully into the town of Sparttul. They had been granted a public audience in the main square by Lord Melville, the Mayor of the town.

The square was packed with people and when Corliss and Jessobelle mounted a small stage, silence fell over the crowd.

"Ladies and gentlemen; thank you for having us here today. I am Prince Corliss of Edomite, and I stand before you today to share something with you. I would not be here, were it not for a witch!"

There were murmurs and whispers in the crowd.

"Indeed! *This* woman!"

Somebody called out from the crowd.

"A witch, you say?"

"Yes; she saved my life! Her name is Jessobelle; she is the head of the Marshwind Coven! No doubt you have heard of them!"

"The Marshwind Witches!" someone shouted. "They are murderers!"

The crowd was stirring now.

"Wrong!" said Corliss. "They are *white* witches, not *black*. Their spells are used for healing! I ask you to let them demonstrate those healing powers today!"

More murmurs from the crowd, but there were no more cries of '*murderers*'.

Suddenly a young woman mounted the platform, carrying an infant. She looked desperately at Jessobelle.

"My baby is sick!" she said. "There is no cure. Can you heal my child?"

Jessobelle took the baby in her arms. She placed her hand on the child's forehead and whispered a few words to it. The infant almost immediately began waving its hands and giggling. The woman gasped; she took the baby back and appeared to be examining it for signs of ailment. When she found none, she screamed with joy.

"My baby!" she cried. "She's healed my baby! It worked; it worked!"

The crowd went wild. Other people now began to come forward; a man with a crutch; an old woman who was blind in one eye. The rest of the witches began mingling; touching people's faces or blowing on physical injuries.

Corliss detached himself from the throng, and quietly walked away. He had a strange sensation that something which had begun years ago, had now been completed.

190

Five days later Corliss arrived back at the city gates. It was early morning; and his birthday. He had used his golden compass to make sure he did not lose his way and now he stood looking at the 'back door' of Edomite, a powerful emotion in his breast.

But it was not the feeling that he usually felt when returning to his father's city; it was bitterness; he was consumed by it. Bitterness that he was returning home without his childhood friend. Everything had changed since the last time he stood here; his innocence for one.

The gates suddenly began to open inwards. And there was his father. They looked at each other for a long time without speaking. Corliss did not move.

"Good morning, my son; you have returned!"

"Yes, Father."

"But where is Ahab?"

Corliss did not immediately reply.

"Ahab is lost!"

The king lowered his head.

"I am so sorry."

Corliss walked in over the threshold. He delved into his bag and removed the book.

"I believe this is what you wanted."

The king took the book from him. As Corliss walked away, the king said, "Yet another prince who has succeeded in his challenge."

Corliss turned back. "I am not a prince, father. Do not call me that ever again!"

He decided that his heart was too troubled to seek out Mariah immediately; he would rest and see her that evening.

Indeed he slept all day; the banquet was to be in the evening, and although he had no interest in it, he would need the energy. He rose two hours before, half expecting Ahab to be there with his glass of wine and bathrobe. Instead, there was another servant in his place.

"Your bath is ready, sire!" said the man, pleasantly.

Corliss simply took the bathrobe and the wine from him and said, "That'll be all!"

He lay in the marble tub for an hour, trying to think of nothing. But that was impossible.

The banqueting hall was decked out in stunning fashion; over two hundred people were there, for no other reason than to celebrate the prince's twenty-first birthday. The only person who didn't feel like celebrating, was Corliss himself. However, when Mariah arrived in a beautiful evening gown, he knew that his love for her was undiminished and he vowed to himself that, despite everything, they would have a happy future together.

He was placed next to his father and Mariah in front of the enormous fireplace. He tried to smile cordially at everybody who wished him happy birthday; tried to pretend that everything was normal. But it felt as though nobody really cared; as if Ahab had never actually existed or was of any importance. Whereas, to Corliss, he was the most important element he could think of at that moment and always had been. It was Ahab who should be sitting where he was now, and not Corliss; he felt like an imposter. He understood how Araznus must have felt; or rather, how *he* must have felt, *as* Araznus. And so he knew he had something else in common with Ahab; they had both felt injustice and hatred, terrible burdens experienced in The Land Beyond.

A cowed figure suddenly appeared at his side and laid a plate of food before him. Corliss barely felt like eating, though he *was* hungry. He picked up his cutlery and began eating slowly.

He listened, throughout the banquet, to speeches being made about him; he listened as the king praised his courage and strength to venture into The Land Beyond. Here, Corliss clenched his fists and stared into his goblet of wine, which the servant kept replenishing.

When his father sat down after having made his speech, he turned to Corliss and said,

"You are upset, my boy. Tell me why?"

"Isn't it obvious, Father?" replied Corliss, through clenched teeth.

The king patted him on the back.

"Let us excuse ourselves from the table; I have something I want to show you."

Through a curtained door in the wall, they left the banqueting hall and entered a small library. There was a desk with two candelabras and on it the book, which Corliss had been sent to fetch.

"I am not in the mood, Father!" he said, bluntly. "As far as I'm concerned, I've done what you've asked me to do; I'm not interested in what that book has to tell me; not anymore."

The door suddenly opened, and the cowed figure appeared again with a fresh goblet.

"I do not require any more wine!" snapped Corliss.

The servant stepped back.

"Come, Corliss; take a look; if not for yourself, then for me."

"For *you*?" repeated Corliss, his voice filled with bitterness. "I've done enough for *you*; why should I do anything more?"

The king opened the book.

"Come," he said, again.

His tone was calm, patient. Corliss reluctantly moved forward and glanced casually at the first page. He looked again. What caught his attention was not his name, written in bold letters in the middle of the page, but the fact that the hand in which it was written, was his own. He frowned. "What is this?" he asked.

"See for yourself," said the king.

Corliss turned over the page. He read the heading at the top of it; MY OWN ADVENTURE.

"My *adventure*!"

And as he read, he felt a strange tingle begin to travel down the length of his body. He turned page after page, reading swiftly, energetically; his heart pounded at the same speed. His writing was neat and beautifully formed, as though he had taken his time over it.

"I don't understand; everything here is…" He looked up at his father, who was standing, smiling at him. "Everything that is written here…it is a step by step account of…my *journey*!" He looked back at the book. "The journey I have just taken!" He shook his head. "But I wrote this! When did I…"

"A long time ago!" said his father, laying a hand on his shoulder. "Do you understand?" he asked.

"Understand; I understand none of it!"

"My dear, Corliss; you *planned* this journey yourself. You planned every detail! Who you would meet along the way, who would help you and who would hinder you; which route you would take, what perils you would face.

The witches, for example, are old friends of yours; you wanted to help them as much as they wanted to help you."

"Planned it!" He was breathing hard. "Why would I plan to fall out with my best friend; why would I plan to almost fall to my death, or to be ambushed by robbers and attacked by mountain lions? Tell me father why...why would I *do* that?"

"To *learn*, Corliss; to *learn*! It's like what I said with the apple; each apple tree grows with knowledge. *We* are the apple trees, Corliss; we stand in our orchards, surrounded by other trees. And yet we are so much more than just wood; we are the apples that grow on our branches. You are not just Corliss, my son; you are Araznus, you are Ulysses; you are Benjamin; you are a hundred other personalities. In each of these personalities you have acquired knowledge and understanding; and with all this knowledge, you will reach where *I* am! One day when you have acquired enough knowledge, you will no longer need to search."

"Are you telling me...are you telling me that I planned for my best friend to die?"

"No!"

"That was *my* decision," said the servant who was still lingering near the door.

Corliss turned and saw the figure draw back its hood.

"It can't be!" whispered Corliss.

Ahab's smile was as rich as it had ever been.

"Hello, my friend!"

Corliss knelt at his feet and sobbed. Ahab knelt down with him. The two men held each other for a long time.

"You are alive!" said Corliss, over and over.

"I am alive!" replied Ahab.

"But you fell! You fell!"

"But not to my death," replied Ahab.

"Forgive me!"

"There is nothing to forgive, Corliss. We were simply exploring the different aspects of our friendship! We have explored them before, as Araznus and Balthazar.

I have more knowledge than you, Corliss, and you wanted to know as much as me. I decided to help you this time, to achieve that. So we swapped roles; I would play the angry, jealous one, and you could experience what I experienced as Balthazar. But you did not want to kill me again, so it had to be an accident. By dying, I would force you to find your inner strength and courage, and therefore teach you about loss, loneliness, faith, friendship, guilt and bravery. As for me, I crave knowledge; I always have. I want to feel every emotion there is, even the negative ones. I love you, Corliss, but sometimes I feel that I don't fully appreciate that. If I can experience the extreme contrasts to that love, *then* I can appreciate it fully. What we have here in Amal is all love and happiness; when we enter The Land Beyond, we see and feel the opposite."

Corliss nodded slowly, tears rolling down his face.

"And the room?" he asked. "What is that? *Where* is that?"

"The room is where you wrote this book; it is where you plan your challenges. This challenge was simply to show you that you need have no fear of The Land Beyond, because it is entirely up to you what happens there. The room is part of who you truly are; that is why you remember it."

"Hence, I remembered the waterfall and the plan I had written."

"Precisely. As to *where* the room is; that is simple. It is just one room out of many; the rooms that span the circumference of the concert hall!"

Corliss smiled.

"The doors that do not open!" He nodded. "Of course! That is why I feel so at home in that place." Corliss rose to his feet. "And what of the next book, the one that details what will happen to Mariah and me if we go back to The Land Beyond? Where is *that* book?"

"Safely stored away!" said his father, smiling.

Mariah was walking in the palace gardens when two people approached her. She recognised them immediately, but there was something different about them. Corliss and Ahab stood before her. However, Corliss was no longer dressed as a prince but in traditional servant's costume, which Ahab usually wore.

"Corliss!" she exclaimed.

He smiled. "There is something which I need to explain to you."

Mariah listened quietly as Corliss told her the truth about himself and Ahab.

"I am aware that this may come as a shock but…"

He turned suddenly to Ahab. "Could I have a moment alone, please?"

Without a word, Ahab removed himself from their company. Corliss stared at Mariah.

"I hope, my darling Mariah, that you can still love me, even though I am just a servant."

"My sweet Corliss," she began, "you are who you are. And who you are, and always have been, is Corliss the person; not Corliss the prince, now Corliss the servant. I am in love with you; a change in role or rank could never alter my affections."

She kissed him and they embraced.

"I was so worried," sighed Corliss, "worried that you would not love me anymore. I will never keep secrets from you again."

"One question then," said Mariah, standing back from him. "Now that you are no longer the prince of Edomite, do we still have to make our trip to The Land Beyond?"

"Now that," replied Corliss, "is a very good question."

Ahab and Corliss found themselves floating down the river on a food boat, their feet dangling in the moonlit water. They sat with their arms around each other's shoulders, like two boys on an adventure. It was a warm night.

"Look at those stars!" said Corliss. "There are so many of them."

"Do you remember what I once told you?" asked Ahab.

"What was that?"

"The reason the stars shine so bright is because each star belongs to a *soul*."

"A soul?" asked Corliss.

"The apple tree."

Corliss nodded, understanding.

"In that star is just a fraction of the energy and knowledge that we have, and yet that is all that is required to keep those stars burning for many years to come. When finally they do die out, we just add another bit of energy to rekindle them. But our friendship, Corliss, will never die; because we are always adding to it!"

Corliss smiled broadly. "Where are we going?" he asked.

"Ah," said Ahab, with a wink. "That's my surprise!"

Chapter Twenty-Three

A New Understanding

Moses paused. He took a long, deep breath and smiled at Jamie.

"The end!"

Jamie sighed; he smiled back at the gypsy.

"Now, do you understand?"

Jamie opened his mouth to speak, and then stopped.

"Yes, some of it," he said.

Again, Moses took a long deep breath in, as if he were thinking about how to phrase something.

"To put it in the most basic terms, what you are going through now with your father is a challenge that you already chose. That is what we, as souls, do. We come here to this world to challenge ourselves, and as the king said, to *learn*! We write our own lives, we create our own fiction! Because that is what life is; it's like a book, where we play fictitious characters. But we are the authors of that book."

"But why?" asked Jamie. "Why did I choose this?"

"It is always based on love, Jamie. Who is there in your family that you want to love? Or to be loved by?"

Jamie wiped a tear from his eye.

"My sister," he said, quietly. "We had an argument. It was she who told me about my dad. I never used to get on with her, she would always be mean to me. But she said she was sorry and that I was the best thing in the family; even though I'm an outsider." He started to cry. "But I didn't listen to her. I ran away! It was the first time she had ever been nice to me. I thought she hated me, but she doesn't." He looked up at Moses. "Do you think that I have known her before?"

"Yes!" replied Moses. "I think you have known her before, but in what capacity, I don't know. You may have known her many times."

The horse whinnied quietly. Moses glanced over at him.

"Mojo's feeling lonely!" he said, chuckling.

They went over to speak to him.

"Like Ahab, people will do things for your character; things that will help. Ahab died so that Corliss would be forced to cope on his own, which is what he wanted. Perhaps your father is helping to strengthen the bond between you and your sister." Moses stroked Mojo's nose. "Have you ever heard the phrase, *every cloud has a silver lining*?"

Jamie nodded. "What does it mean?"

"It means that for every *bad* thing that happens, there is always something *good* that comes out of it. The Christian God says, *love your enemies*; because they are *not* your enemies, they are your best friends! It's like the Fire Spirit said, you should not be afraid of the things that you fear, because fear is an illusion. There is no danger, and there is no pain.

"Ahab was bitter towards Corliss because they argued and they had killed each other in the past, but they were just pretending. Because at the end of the day, no one really gets hurt. Like a piece of theatre where two characters fight; it's all beautifully choreographed, and

200

when it's all over, the actors stand side by side and take their bows!"

Jamie nodded, quietly.

"And there is always someone to help you along the way. Jessobelle with her ring, for example; or in your case, the school psychologist. Jessobelle was a seer, like my mother; they can give you advice from what are called Spirit Guides; like the Fire Spirit; and you can talk to these spirits whenever you want; they are always listening."

"Can you hear them?" asked Jamie.

"They give you signs, things that may be obscure to someone else, but which will mean something to you." Moses smiled. "You are never truly on your own. And then there are those who have already experienced what you have been through, and leave their trail of light behind them for you to follow. Like the person who left food in the cave for Corliss. When you're walking through a dark forest at night, it's easier to find your way, when that way is illuminated." He patted the horse.

"My mother had a wonderful gift; but there are many in this world who possess that gift; possess the ability to see a little further than others; such as the Tree Dwellers; they have a different view. And once you know that life is your own design, you can then just get on with it; like the people in the sinking houses. Ultimately, wisdom and understanding will bring inner peace."

Jamie looked at his watch.

"I better go," he said. "Thank you."

"Well, it was very nice to meet you, Jamie. And I hope that I have helped in some way."

As they shook hands, Moses added, "Look out for the signs. They are different for everybody, but you will know them when you see them."

Chapter Twenty-Four

Back with the Family

Jamie walked slowly back towards their caravan; he knew he would be in for a bollocking for disappearing so long.

He thought about the story he had just listened to and about the gypsy who had told it to him. What an extraordinary meeting; and what an extraordinary person. He felt strange, as though he had taken some sort of medicine.

"Jamie!"

Jamie had been looking at his feet; he now snapped his head up as he recognised Bob's booming voice.

"Jamie!"

Bob actually ran towards him; something he had never seen him do before, and he never knew Bob could move that fast. Jamie stopped short. He was in trouble now. But Bob didn't appear to be his usual angry self, and the tone in which he shouted Jamie's name sounded more like joy. He jumped over a small flower bed in his eagerness to reach the boy and came thundering over the grass. By now he was out of breath. He came to a standstill a yard from Jamie. The two of them stood, looking at each other.

"Jamie!" said Bob, again.

Jamie locked eyes with him; he didn't move.

"Where have you been?" asked Bob, his tone uneasy.

"I've been by myself."

Bob nodded, slowly. He was nervous and fidgety.

"You, er…you okay?"

"I'm fine."

Bob came up to him. He laid a fat hand on his shoulder.

"Jamie…" he began.

But Jamie cut him off.

"Why didn't you tell me that you weren't my real dad?"

Bob stared at him and removed his hand.

"I…How do you…"

"Lauren told me! Why didn't you? You must have been *dying* to?"

Bob lowered his head. And then he did something that surprised Jamie more than anything that had happened that evening; he burst into tears. He crumpled to the ground in front of the boy and put his head in his hands.

"I'm sorry!" he sobbed.

Jamie didn't know what to do. At first he thought Bob must be drunk, as he stood looking down at this quivering wreck that he had feared his entire life. Bob reached out for Jamie, but Jamie didn't go to him.

"What are you sorry for? Are you sorry that you hurt me? Are you sorry that you've never said a civil word to me until now? What are you sorry for…*Bob*?"

Bob looked up into the boy's face. His expression and his sincerity were, in that moment, utterly real.

"I've hurt you so much, Jamie. I've lied to you and I said I didn't love you. But I do. I love you to bits, Jamie. You're a wonderful boy, but you're not my son. You're somebody else's. Don't you get it? I'm jealous of that, and I wish you were *mine*! I wish someone as perfect as you, came from someone as *shitty* as *me*!"

Jamie was crying now, too. He dropped to the ground and flung his arms around Bob, burying his face in that

203

enormous shoulder. Bob kissed him and held onto him as if he would never let him go again.

"I love you so much, Jamie. I love you all; your mum, your sister!" He suddenly pulled away and looked Jamie square in the eyes. "Jamie, it's Lauren!" he said, desperately.

Jamie ran towards his mother.

"Where is she?"

"Jamie, calm down, she's being looked after!"

"Where is she, where's Lauren?"

Elaine took him to see her in the ward. Jamie stared in horror at the unconscious form in the bed before him, hooked up to a monitor. She hardly seemed to be breathing.

"No!" whispered Jamie.

"Sweetheart, it's maybe best that you come away for just now, until she's better. It's only going to upset you, seeing her like this."

"What's wrong with her?"

His mother didn't reply.

"What's wrong with her?" he persisted.

"She took some pills!"

"It's my fault!" cried Jamie.

"No, nothing's your fault, sweetheart…"

"It *is*! I ran away. I told her I didn't believe her!" He ran forward. "I believe you, Lauren! I believe you! It's alright. I forgive you now!"

"Jamie…"

Suddenly the monitor started to emit a long shrill beep.

"Lauren!" shrieked Elaine.

"What's happening?" said Jamie, alarmed.

The white curtain was suddenly yanked open and two nurses and a female doctor rushed in.

"What's wrong?" asked Elaine.

"She's going into cardiac arrest!"

Elaine screamed; Bob ran in.

"Lauren!"

"I need you folks to step back!" said the doctor.

One of the nurses grabbed a set of paddles and began preparing to shock Lauren with them. Elaine was still screaming. The doctor removed her white coat to give herself more flexibility.

"Okay, shock her!"

There was a high-pitched buzzing sound and a second later, Lauren's body gave a sudden jolt as the electricity went to her heart.

"Lauren!" shouted Jamie.

The doctor now started CPR.

"I love you, Lauren; you're my big sister!"

The girl's body gave another jolt. Again the CPR.

"You're my big sister!" sobbed Jamie, again. "I'll always love you; I'll never forget what you said to me in the fairground!" He started screaming now. "Lauren don't you dare die on me! You can't do that!"

Another shock with the paddles and another round of CPR. But the CPR stopped after only a few moments; there was a deafening stillness.

"Lauren?"

The doctor looked up at the nurses. She shook her head.

"There's nothing more we can do; I'm calling it." She looked at her watch. "23:40!"

Jamie stood and stared. His sister lay there; motionless, pale faced...dead. There was a sudden calm; everything went silent. He couldn't hear his parents screaming; he couldn't hear his father calling Lauren's name over and over again. All he heard was his owl, hooting to him in that forest.

"What are you saying to me, Mr. Owl? Are you trying to tell me that everything is under control; that everything is going to be okay? Well you're too late for that! My sister is gone!"

His eyes travelled up from Lauren's face, up the pale green wall towards the ceiling, as if he would see her spirit hovering there. But instead he found himself looking at the decor. This was the Young Person's Ward and there were images of animals and birds painted on the wall.

And there it was; even through the tears that blurred his vision, he could see it as plain as day. Sitting on a branch, looking directly down at the bed in which his sister lay, was a beautiful white barn owl!

Without thinking what he was doing, Jamie rushed forward and leapt onto the bed.

"Look, Lauren!" he shrieked. "It's my *barn owl*!" He began hammering away on her chest like some possessed maniac. *"You've got to be okay*! It's a *sign*!"

His mother dragged him off the bed.

"Shock her again!" he screamed at the doctor.

"Listen…!" began the doctor.

"Just do it!" he yelled, at the top of his lungs.

The doctor looked perplexed. Then she said; "Give it one more go!"

The nurse charged up the paddles once again.

"Shock her!"

Lauren's body arched with the electricity. They waited; nothing. Jamie closed his eyes. And it was at that moment that he heard the noise; the beep, beep, beep of a regular heartbeat.

The curtains were closed once more; Bob, Elaine and Jamie sat round Lauren's bed. Elaine held a ragged tissue, soaked through with tears; Bob was motionless, he just stared at his beloved daughter, feeling completely helpless; and Jamie was deep in his own thoughts.

"How are we going to survive?" he asked, suddenly.

Elaine stirred.

"What was that, sweetie?"

"I said, how are we going to survive; as a family, I mean?"

Bob sighed heavily, but said nothing.

"We'll just have to do our best, won't we?" said Elaine.

"We need to learn to talk to each other properly. We need to be civil and no more arguing!" He looked at Bob as he said this. "No more sitting down in front of the telly and stuffing your face with chips and beer, while Lauren sits with her phone up in her room. You do realise that other families sit round a dinner table together most nights?"

"We don't have a dinner table!" muttered Bob.

"Then stop smoking so many cigarettes and buy one! Go to the gym once in a while, Bob! Take your doctor seriously; otherwise sooner or later it's going to be you in that bed!" replied Elaine.

"And Mum, you need to go back to the clinic! We could have lost Lauren; I thought we had. My sister's very sick. She even took ecstasy to try and make herself feel better because she hates her life! What if Lauren has serious health complications because of that? Is this what's finally going to sort this family out?"

Jamie rushed out of the cubicle. Elaine looked over at her husband.

"He's right, Bob."

"I know he's right. He's a bright little spark that boy." He took her hand, but didn't manage to look at her. "I've been a bad husband to you, Elaine; and a bad father to Jamie. I can't take back what I've done to him; I can't reverse this." He waved a hand towards Lauren. "But I *can* turn it around from now on!" He looked at her, his eyes filled with determination. "I promise you, Elaine; I'm going to do right by you and our children. The first thing I'll do when we get back is buy a dining table."

Elaine actually laughed but only momentarily.

"It's going to take a lot more than a dining table to sort out our family, Bob."

He nodded.

"Of course it is. But you know what they say; one step at a time!"

Two days later, Lauren was still unconscious, but she seemed to be stable for now. Jamie was sitting by her bedside; he'd hardly left it. Bob and Elaine were having a meeting with the doctor. The ward was relatively quiet, apart from the regular sounds of nurses and medicine trolleys.

Suddenly Lauren moved. Jamie's heart jumped, and he leaped forward.

"Lauren?"

She opened her eyes, blinked several times and then looked at Jamie. She looked dazed and confused.

"Lauren, it's me, Jamie!"

"I know who you are, dummy!"

Jamie started to laugh and cry at the same time.

"You're okay!"

"Where am I?"

"You're in the hospital. You collapsed."

"Shit! Are Mum and Dad here?"

Jamie nodded.

"Shit! What was it? The ecstasy?"

"Yea." Jamie started to cry properly now. "Don't ever do something like that again! Do you hear me? Never again!"

Lauren reached up a hand and brushed a tear from his cheek.

"I promise," she said, matter-of-factly.

She took hold of Jamie's hand and squeezed it.

"Hey, come on, don't get wimpy on me!"

She smiled at him. He wiped his eyes and smiled back.

"I want to tell you something," she said. "I had a strange dream about you. We were in a hot country. I wasn't well, and you were holding me in your arms and crying. You were so distraught. I knew I was either dead or dying, but it was like I was watching it from outside of my body, like I wasn't really there. You were telling me you loved me. You were saying it was your fault. And I wanted to tell you that it wasn't, but I couldn't speak."

Jamie lowered his head. "I ran away from you in the fair. I should have stayed. I'm sorry…"

"Jamie, don't. Don't say that. You've got nothing to apologise for! I don't care where you come from or whose child you are; you're my little brother. I'll always love you, and I'll always be there for you."

Jamie couldn't hold back the tears.

"And I'll always be there for *you*!" he said.

He leaned down and hugged his sister. "When you get better, I want to take you to see somebody. His name is Moses and he's a new friend of mine. I want you to hear what he has to say because it's very important. Alright?"

She nodded. "Alright."

EPILOGUE

Akina sat in the shade of a tree, where she had dragged her brother's body. She held him so tight in her arms and shook with horror; she was holding nothing more than a corpse.

Her brother was gone. It was her fault; she should never have left him. She would never forgive herself; never.

Her parents were not capable of looking after themselves, let alone their children. Akina and her brother Mojo had been left largely to fend for themselves. Her brother was weak, and she was the strong one. She did her job as an older sister very well. She would lead him around by the hand when he was very young and made sure he stayed away from snakes and other dangers.

When there was no food in the house, she would go to find Takaya, the wise man of the village, and he would give them rice.

She had gone out to find water. Their well had dried up and the sun was baking hot. Mojo was not strong enough to make the journey to the other village, so she had decided to leave him in the house. When she got back, he was gone. Frantically she went searching for him, all round the village. And then, here, on the outskirts, she had found him, lying face down in the sand.

Suddenly she rose, lifted Mojo's body into her arms and walked with him to Takaya's house.

Little Akina stood before Takaya and looked up at him.

"Please help me!" she said, feebly.

Takaya crouched down.

"You are the medicine man. Please wake my brother up."

"Alas, Akina, I do not have the medicines to do that. I am so sorry."

Takaya took Mojo's body from her and laid it down on the floor of his hut. They sat down together and looked at him.

"Death is not the end, Akina. It is merely a parting for a period of time. You will see Mojo again."

"When? Where?"

"In the next world; the one that belongs to the Great Spirit. There you will meet Mojo again. But also in another life from this one. Our lives in this world are short, so we can have many. You can help Mojo again in another life. Let him rest just now."

Tears rolled down Akina's face.

"I want to help him again. I want him to know that I cared for him, that I loved him and that I'm sorry I left him." She stood up. "I will take him to my parents," she said.

But she did not take him home. Instead she went back to the tree. She was still there when the stars twinkled over the village.

"I love you, Mojo; never let me forget that. I love you even more now that you've gone. I want to be reminded of my love for you, and I want to live again with you. I want to save you next time. I'm *going* to save you. And I am going to make sure that mother and father take care of us. I want you to know how much I loved you; I want you to know what happened here today." She closed her eyes. "Goodnight, Mojo. I will see you in the morning."

Takaya stood over the bodies of young Akina and her brother Mojo, as they lay together under the baobab tree; they looked happy, even in death. He crouched down and brushed the hair back out of Akina's face.

"I will see you again, child; in time."

THE END